Nothing to Die For

RICHARD HOUSTON

Version 2022.26.12

Cover Art by GH Design

Edited by Elise Abrams

Thank you to the following beta readers for pointing out plot and typo errors:

Cheryl Houston, George Burke, Patti Saint Marie Wilson, and Jim Bessey

Chapter One

THE CREASE IN JACK Morgan's forehead became more pronounced and inflamed the more he yelled at me. "You're not going to get a better offer, you know," he said after I replied I'd think about it to his offer on my lots. I had bought two lots in one of Truman's so-called resorts a few years back and out of the blue, a local real estate agent had contacted me about selling them. Although he offered me far more than they were worth, I had an ominous feeling about it. The lots were located in a development by the water that had been plated in the fifties. The original lots had been purchased for only a few hundred dollars so fishermen from the Kansas City area could build weekend cabins. My lots were what realtors called second-tier -- not on the water, but close enough that they had a great view, and in the case of mine, a stone's throw to the community docks and boat ramp. It was a location that has seen a lot of interest lately. I'd agreed to meet the realtor that morning. It was a great excuse to put off working on my book.

"Maybe not now, but I have a feeling they will be worth more in a few years. Besides, I may want to build on it myself someday. It's getting harder to find anything this close to the water where there is enough room for a septic system and well."

Jack's nostrils flared. If I wasn't careful, he'd be breathing fire and roast me to death. "I know people who could make it impossible for you to put in a septic system, so I suggest you take my offer. You'll never be able to build on it otherwise." He had raised his right hand pointing his index finger at me.

Fred must have sensed the change in his mood and began to growl.

"Are you threatening me?" I asked as I grabbed Fred's collar.

The realtor retracted his hand and started to rub the back of his neck. "I'm just saying you shouldn't think too long about my offer. I'll call you next week to see if you change your mind." We watched as he waddled over to his shiny new Range Rover and laboriously lifted his heft into the driver's seat before leaving.

Fred and I walked my property after the cloud of acrid blue smoke from the SUV's spinning tires cleared. He stopped to sniff where I'd seen a squirrel scurry up a tree a few minutes earlier. It was near the spot with the best view of the water and where I'd thought about building a home someday if my girlfriend, Kelly, ever married me. But that was looking more like a dream lately.

Was it that long ago when we'd picnicked under the big oak tree and talked about how it would give us the shade we needed from the summer heat and let the warm sun in during the winter? Now that Kelly's mother had a stroke and moved in with her, those dreams were gone, and I had to decide if I should take Morgan's offer and move on with my life. Maybe it was time to grow up and get a real job in the city.

I'm sure my property was worth more than I paid for it, but I didn't know if the realtor's offer had been reasonable or not. Was it enough to buy anything in the city? It would make a nice down payment on something, even if I could qualify for a mortgage. Maybe I should use the money to pay the deposit and first and last month's rent on something until I could figure out what I wanted to do.

Fred got tired of waiting for the squirrel to come out of the tree and picked up a stick and brought it over to me, dropping it at my feet. He sat on his haunches and waited for me to throw it When I finally gave in and threw the stick towards the road at the end of our property, I couldn't help but wonder how he would like being cooped up in a small fenced-in yard if we were to move to the city. That was something he had never experienced. He'd grown up in our mountain cabin back in Colorado and he'd always been able to roam free. Even after moving to Bonnie's homestead here in Missouri, Fred had the freedom to go where he wanted. Did I really want to give up and go back to a back-stabbing office?

The homestead shack I'd fixed up and had been living in for the last few years didn't need any more work and I'd been looking for something to occupy my time. I'd been bored out of my mind since my daughter, Allie, went off to college with her dog and the agreement I had with Bonnie Jones, my neighbor, to fix up her family's homestead in exchange for my home was winding down. The only work I had left was some routine maintenance and keeping Bonnie's family farm's one hundred sixty acres from being overgrown. Even that would be coming to an end soon because Bonnie's sister, the absentee owner of the homestead, was in negotiations with some big corporation to manage the farm. They had convinced her that she was sitting on a goldmine. They would plant some cash crops and split the profit with her.

I knew I should be working on my next book, but I just couldn't seem to get started. Maybe building another house would give me the inspiration I needed, and at the least, it would give me something to do. My lake property would be worth a lot more if it was improved and the proceeds would be more than enough to pay Allie's expenses that weren't covered by scholarships. It should also leave me a comfortable cushion to live off of until I decided to get back to writing.

Fred came back with the stick, dropped it at my feet, and waited for me to throw it again. "Whoa, Freddie," I said, backing up. "Are you back already?" Fred barked and pushed the stick closer to me. But before I could throw it for him again, my cell phone started playing Beethoven.

"What's up, Bon?" I answered after seeing it was Bonnie.

"I'm really worried about Tigger, Jake. She never came home this morning. I'm afraid something has happened to her. Can you and Fred help me look for her? Maybe Freddie can use that great nose of his to find her."

Chapter Two

FRED WAS THE FIRST to hear Tigger's call for help. Her meowing was so weak, I could only assume she'd been at it all night long. She must have sensed her friend was nearby, as only animals can, and made one last desperate call for help.

Bonnie, Fred, and I had been searching abandoned farm houses and barns for the cat after she called me. I hadn't searched in earnest at first because, like most cats that are allowed to come and go as they please, it wasn't unusual for Tigger to stay out all night. She had first gone missing yesterday. Bonnie had spent the day checking her outbuildings and fields before calling me. When Fred and I joined the search, we slowly drove down the road behind Bonnie's family farm and called out at every empty building we could find. Fred picked up the cat's scent after jumping out of my truck at an abandoned farm house. Although there was a new For Sale sign in the yard next to the road, rumor had it that one of our county commissioners, Madeline Summers, was negotiating to sell the house and eighty acres to a company in Kansas City that was buying up old farms. They had a reputation of leveling everything, houses, barns, and outbuildings, so they could grow more soybeans and corn.

Bonnie caught up to us at the front door. "Well, just don't stand there, Jake. Break the door down, so I can get Tigger," she said after catching her breath.

"Don't you think we should call 911?" I had my cellphone in my hand, ready to key in the number.

"Tigger will be dead by the time they get here. Please kick down that door, or get out of the way so I can do it," she said, veins bulging in her neck.

I was worried she'd have a stroke. "Calm down, Bon. There must be a better way. How did Tigger get in? Maybe she climbed through a vent or something," I said, pointing to the small gable vent at the peak of the roof. "Besides, how would I explain breaking and entering to Kelly?"

Bonnie put her hands on her hips and looked at me like I was mentally slow. "It's not breaking and entering if you have probable cause. And you don't need to tell me to calm down. I've got twenty years on you, Sonny, enough time to know the law in cases like this."

I felt like telling her just because she was over seventy, it didn't qualify her as a lawyer but thought better of it. "You've been watching too many crime shows, Bon. We're not cops, but Kelly is, so maybe I should give her a call," I said, turning back to my cellphone.

My phone failed to connect. "Guess it's back to plan B," I said when I saw there was no service and realized Bonnie was right – I'd have to break in if we were going to rescue Tigger before Fred did it for me. All he knew was that the cat he saved as a kitten was inside crying out for help. Now that he had found Tigger, he wanted in and clawed at the front door trying to open it.

The house had been neglected for years. That was apparent by the peeling paint on the clapboard siding and missing roof shingles. There were other things, too, like a lawn that hadn't been cut in months and some broken windows, but Fred didn't pick up on those clues. "Hold on, old boy," I said and broke out a pane of glass in the nine-lite front door so I could reach inside and unlock the deadbolt."

We followed the cat's cry to a room on the far side of the main room. The door wouldn't budge. The doorknob turned but something was stopping me from opening it. I put my shoulder and most of my weight behind it to try to get it to open. It moved an inch, but not enough to get inside. I expected Fred to help and was surprised when he began growling instead. Then I saw why.

"I hope you have a good explanation for breaking that window and forcing your way in here." I gave up trying to push the door open and turned to see a woman standing in the doorway. She looked to be in her early or mid-thirties with dishwater-blonde hair tied off in a pony tail. The jeans and KC Chief's sweatshirt she was wearing were well worn as though she had used them for gardening.

Bonnie yelped and turned, too. Like me, she had been so intent on getting the door opened, she hadn't heard the woman come up the porch stairs. She drew herself to her full height of five feet, three inches before answering. "My cat is trapped in there and can't get out," she said.

The stranger glanced at the cell phone in her hand, then waved it like a weapon. "Yeah, right. You can tell it to the police when they get here. I called 911 and gave them your license plate before confronting you, so don't even think of doing anything because they will be here soon." Even with the scowl on her face, the woman was attractive in a tomboy sort of way, until I realized her torn jeans were made that way. She no sooner finished her rant, than a familiar face came into the room.

"I should have known you three would be involved," said a voice I knew all too well. I turned toward Kelly who was standing four feet away with her arms crossed. Fred went over to greet her, forgetting about his trapped friend for the moment.

Bonnie's posture slumped again. "Fred found Tigger in there. We were only trying to rescue her. It's not like we caused any damage. They're going to level this place anyway," Bonnie said, without looking Kelly in the eyes.

Kelly sighed, uncrossed her arms, and walked over to the stranger. "Unfortunately, I can vouch for them, Stephanie. Bonnie's cat has been missing for several days. I'm sure they meant no harm."

The way Kelly talked to the woman, told me she knew her personally and not just from calling 911. "No harm, no foul, Deputy Brown, but the old gal is wrong about leveling the house. Despite my objections, mom has decided to just sell the farm and keep the house in the family. That's why I was checking on the old place. To see what needs to be done before moving in."

"So, you're Madeline Summers's daughter?" I asked.

She was slow to nod. "Stephanie Travers. And you two are?"

"I hate to break up your little chat, but Tigger is still trapped in that room," Bonnie broke in.

Stephanie frowned and put the cell phone she'd been holding back in her pocket. "Of course. Let me help you push that door open."

"Not in your condition," Bonnie said, pointing to the bulge in Stephanie's stomach that I hadn't noticed because of her sweatshirt.

The three of us, Kelly, Bonnie, and myself, put our shoulders to the door and pushed. The extra weight was all we needed to make the door open a crack. Fred managed to get through the small opening and barked.

"What'd you find, Fred," I called out.

He barked again and Tigger squeezed out of the crack in the doorway. She ran over to Bonnie and jumped into her arms. "Oh, my poor baby. Are you hurt?" She had tears in her eyes as she turned away from us and took Tigger outside.

The crack in the doorway wasn't big enough for us to squeeze in but large enough for us to smell something dead.

The odor coming from the room was terrible. "Tigger must have chased a squirrel in there and killed it," I said, holding a hand to my nose.

Kelly tried pushing on the door some more, then gave up when it wouldn't budge and reached for her radio. "Whatever is blocking the door must be heavy. I better call for help."

"I have a better idea," I said and went into the dining room. I took one of the oak leaves from the dining room table and returned to the door. Kelly had put her radio back on her shoulder and shrugged while shaking her head.

"Archimedes," I said, putting one end of the leaf into the crack of the door. "Give him a lever long enough and he said he could move the world. All I need is one long enough to move a door."

Kelly grinned and her lips turned into a wide smile. "Mac-Gyver to the rescue," she said as the door opened revealing the back of a huge dresser.

"Wait here until we move the dresser," Kelly said to Stephanie. I'd only managed to move the door enough for Kelly and me to squeeze through. I flipped the light switch on the wall next to the door and nothing happened.

"The power hasn't been on for years," Stephanie said when she saw me flip the switch. We couldn't see beyond the dresser. The only light in the room came from the living room windows. I reached for my cellphone and turned on its flashlight.

Fred's eyes lit up like two red dots. It must have been what Cerberus looked like to Hercules, except Fred only had one head and one set of eyes. When I saw a window on the far wall, I walked over and pulled back the drapes. I noticed that the lock at the top of the bottom pane was in the closed position and by the amount of undisturbed dust on it, it didn't look like it had been opened in ages.

The bedroom looked like it was once a den or study, but it could have also been a library at one time. One wall was covered with an ornate, mahogany built-in bookcase that only a skilled craftsman could have made. I spotted a space heater plugged into a wall outlet next to where the dresser had been and wondered if the furnace had broken down. Then I realized it must run on propane which had run out years ago.

Fred was at the side of a four-poster bed, carved with the same care as the bookcase. Now that we could see without the dim light of my cellphone, we knew what had Fred so upset. There was a dead body lying on the bed.

Kelly didn't have to check the pulse of the corpse because even Mister Magoo could see the woman was dead. Her brains were plastered all over the headboard. An old revolver she had shot herself with was still in her right hand.

Fred came over to my side and sat. He looked up at me smiling like he expected me to say something nice or pat him on the head. I chose the latter.

Kelly simply stared at the body. "My God, she's our county commissioner, Madeline Summers."

"Mother?" Stephanie said, wide-eyed.

"Kelly nodded her head. "You need to take Stephanie out of this room, Jake, and don't touch anything. I'm going to have a hard time explaining why civilians are contaminating our crime scene."

Stephanie looked at Kelly like she just said the F word. "I'm a big girl and why do you think this is a crime scene? Unless the murderer can walk through walls, it kinda looks like suicide to me. There is no way anyone could have blocked the door with that dresser and left the room."

"We better go, Stephanie, and let Kelly do her work," I said taking her elbow and leading her from the room. I wanted to ask why the power was out if Madeline Summers had been using the bedroom. Evidently, she had been using the space heater to keep warm but it required electricity. Something didn't add up.

Chapter Three

KELLY WAS TALKING TO Stephanie in her patrol car when Sheriff Bennett showed up with the coroner. He took one look at Bonnie, Fred, and me then scowled before going into the house where Maddie was taking her final nap. After a few minutes, he summoned all of us into the living room. The fact that her mother was dead must have caught up with Stephanie. Bonnie and Kelly went over to where she was now sitting on an antique loveseat with her head in her hands. I didn't have a clue what to say to a woman who just lost her mother, so I held on to my dog to keep him away from the front door with broken glass.

"Kelly tells me you and Mrs. Jones broke into the house to rescue her cat. Do you have any idea how the cat got locked up in there?" Bennett asked in a flat monotone voice as the coroner was removing the body.

"The only theory I can think of is that Tigger must have been in the room when Maddie killed herself. The only way in and out of that room is through the bedroom door as far as I can tell. Maddie must have tipped over the dresser before she shot herself with Tigger in there. I have no idea what the cat was doing here unless Mrs. Summers picked her up thinking she was a stray."

Bennett let out a deep breath and nodded. "That's what I thought, too. She was always taking in stray cats and dogs."

He glanced down at a notepad he held in one hand then looked up at me, shaking his head. His eyes were wet and dull, showing emotion I'd never seen in him before. "Of course, I'll have to wait on the GSR test to confirm gunshot residue on her hand but it's suicide if I ever saw one. There is no way anyone could have left the room after shooting Maddie."

"That's what I thought, too, Sheriff but I wonder why she did it? Did you find a note?"

"You know I can't discuss an open case with civilians, Jake. Please stay out of this one. There's nothing for you here."

Bonnie had left Stephanie and Kelly to join us when she heard us talking about the commissioner. She had been silent until the sheriff told me to keep out of his investigation. "I'm sorry for your loss, Sheriff. I know she was more than a boss to you," she said, placing her hands on her hips as if to dare him to deny it.

Bennett jerked his head as if he'd just noticed her. "Where did you hear that? I hope your church friends aren't gossiping again."

"We don't gossip." Bonnie stood as though she was trying to look taller. "For your information, it's no secret about the two of you. Everyone in town was on to you."

Bennett grimaced, then turned toward Kelly. "I have to notify the state cops. Finish up here and get these people and that dog out of here," he said as he left the room shaking his head.

Stephanie followed Bennett and the coroner outside. I could see her tap the sheriff on the shoulder so she could talk to him, but I couldn't hear what she had to say. A few minutes later, they both got in their cars to leave.

Kelly waited for the sound of Bennett's SUV crunching the gravel in the driveway to subside before speaking. She looked sternly at Bonnie. "What did you say that for? Can't you see he's upset?"

Bonnie lowered her eyes, looking at her feet like she had two different socks on. "I was only trying to make him feel better but it's the truth. Everyone knows he and Maddie were sleeping together." Then she jerked her head up, thrusting out her chin. "But I know when I'm not wanted," she said before picking up Tigger and storming out the door.

"Now she's pissed at me, too," Kelly said. "I don't know why I try. I'm damned if I do and damned if I don't."

I could see there was more than Bonnie bothering her, but she never was one to share her feelings. I guess that's what made her a good cop. Fred must have sensed it, too. He went over to her side and rubbed up against her leg.

She looked down at him while putting a hand on his head. A small smile formed on her lips as she patted him on the head.

"How's Stephanie taking it? I imagine it's quite a shock to her," I asked, trying to change the subject.

"Better than I thought she would. She said her mother's been depressed lately and was afraid she'd do something like this. And by the way, she said she won't press charges for you breaking and entering if you replace the glass you broke."

I took a step back. I started to say something about rescuing Tigger but held it in. "Well, Fred and I better try to catch up with Bonnie. You know how stubborn she can be, she's probably walking home instead of waiting in my truck," I said, then headed for the door.

I should have stayed and tried to see what was bothering Kelly, but that would have meant she'd have to disobey her boss's orders. I sucked when it came to understanding women. I always ended up saying the wrong thing and making matters worse. I probably should have left Fred with her. He seemed to be better at it than I was, but Bennett had wanted him out, too.

My fear that Bonnie had tried to walk home was allayed when I saw her sitting in my truck, pouting. "Sorry about that, Bon," I said as I opened my door, and moved my front seat forward so Fred could climb in the back seat of the truck's extended cab.

"It's no big secret, Jake," she said crossing her arms. "Everyone knows he was sleeping with the commissioner. What I said shouldn't upset Kelly."

I got into the driver's seat and started the truck. "I'm sure it's not anything you said. Something's bothering Kelly and you were in the wrong place at the wrong time," I answered, glancing in my rearview mirror. Fred wasn't a happy camper and I'm sure if he could talk, he'd tell Bonnie that she was in his seat. Fred almost always rode shotgun.

Bonnie's face softened and she reached over to touch my arm. "Lover's quarrel?" she asked.

I felt my face warm up. I'm sure if I could have seen it in the mirror, it would be red. "Bonnie!"

"Well, I'm not exactly blind, you know. Even Homer could tell you two haven't been Romeo and Juliet lately."

I assumed she was referring to the blind, Greek poet and the lovers in Shakespeare's tragedy. It amazed me how she could see these things, and mix her metaphors. I suppose she had her share of lover's quarrels in her seventy-plus years, but opening up to her would be like sharing my love life with my mother. I counted to ten before answering. "Work's been hard on her lately, so I've been giving her some space to work it out. How about we talk about something else or not at all?"

"Do you really think she killed herself?" Bonnie asked as though she hadn't just put her nose where it didn't belong.

"What else can it be? There was no way in or out of that room. The window was locked and there was dust on the sill. If someone had gone out that way, there would have been a trace of it in the dust and those windows can't be locked from outside."

"Don't forget the tallboy," she said, nodding her head.

"Tallboy?"

"The dresser, silly. That's what you call those tall chests of drawers. She must have knocked it over to block the door. There is no way someone could have done that from outside the room," she answered. "However..."

I couldn't see her expression as I had my eyes focused on the narrow county road. One false move and the truck would be in a deep drainage ditch. I could only imagine the wide-eyed stare on her face when she had a revelation. "However?"

"The rumor at church is that Maddie couldn't wait to be a grandmother. Stephanie is in the family way. I find it hard to believe she'd end her life right now. I don't know how Bennett is going to break it to him."

I didn't know which surprised me more, her way of saying Stephanie was pregnant, the belief that Bennett and Madeline Summers were having an affair, or Bonnie's use of pronouns.

"Him? Who is him?"

"Jake. Don't you listen to anything I say? Maddie's husband, not her daughter's. But then the husband is always the last to know, isn't he?"

"Maddie has a husband?" All of a sudden, I had visions of walking in on my ex and what I thought was my best friend.

She sighed and I imagined a smirk on her face. "It's why her affair with the sheriff is so scandalous, or maybe he's the reason for the affair. Rose thinks being a big-shot salesman, always on the road for those Fortune 500 companies is the reason they are separated and will probably get divorced."

"So, you're saying she felt neglected? Maybe it caused her to be depressed. That's usually why people take their own lives."

I still couldn't take my eyes off the road, but my peripheral vision saw her shaking her head. "Rumor has it she wanted a divorce. Does that sound like she's depressed? We need to find out where he was when Maddie was murdered."

"There's no evidence of that. At least not until the coroner comes back with the gunshot residue test. If it comes back negative, then it will more than likely mean the scene was staged and we're looking at murder, but right now, my money's on suicide," I said.

I turned on to the main road and had a chance to look over at Bonnie. The lines on her forehead told me her mind was still thinking about the crime scene – if that's what it was. "I saw that on one of my crime shows. When someone shoots a gun, it always leaves residue on their hand. Right?" she said.

"Unless they are wearing gloves, but I doubt if Maddie could have removed and disposed of gloves after shooting herself."

"Or pushed the highboy over," Bonnie said. She was shaking her head now. "Let me know when the test comes back, Jake. I'll be wondering how anyone could have shot her and got out of the room until you let me know."

"You'll be the first to know. That is, right after Fred because he never misses a thing. Right, old boy?" I said after reaching over the front seat to rub his head. Fred raised his head and even Tigger stood up from where she'd been lying on Bonnie's lap when we turned down the gravel drive leading to Bonnie's house and my little house.

Chapter Four

KELLY CALLED ME THE next morning sounding down. I knew something was wrong so I asked her to meet me for coffee. I'd suggested the only place in town I knew of that was dog friendly.

We beat her to Fido's Coffee and took Fred's favorite table by a large window at the east side of the café. He liked to put his head on the window's wide sill while pretending he was on guard duty. I knew better though; he wouldn't witness any crimes with his eyes closed. He had fallen asleep seconds after the server brought my coffee when he saw I hadn't ordered anything tasty.

I knew Kelly had arrived when Fred raised his head and sat up. "No wonder I never see a cop taking pictures of speeders around here. They're all on coffee breaks," I said and immediately regretted my attempt at humor when I saw the sour expression on her face.

She didn't laugh or even smile at my joke. "Six years in this department and he has the nerve to put one of his few sergeants on traffic. He can take that radar gun and stick it where the sun don't shine for all I care."

Fred must have sensed her mood as well. He sat next to her and put his head in her lap. It made us both smile.

Before I could say anything, a man at the next table gave us a sarcastic look and mumbled under his breath to the woman sitting opposite him, "I guess they don't have a health code in this town." She couldn't look at us and lowered her eyes to study their table.

"He's a service animal," Kelly lied. Her expression changed as though someone had poured cold water on her. "Not that it matters. He'd be allowed in here anyway. It's a pet-friendly establishment."

Grumpy didn't argue. Kelly's uniform had that effect on people but he did get up from his table to say to the woman across from him, "Let's go, Mary, before we get fleas with our coffee." Mary kept her head down and wouldn't look our way as she followed him toward the door. I couldn't help but notice that Grumpy didn't leave a tip.

"That about sums up the day I'm having," Kelly said as we watched the couple go out the door. "Sometimes, it doesn't pay to get out of bed in the morning."

"I know what you mean. It's the way I felt yesterday after meeting Jack Morgan. Talk about a strange conversation."

Kelly's eyes lit up at the mention of the man responsible for the recent budget cuts, including funding for the sheriff's department. "Our county commissioner?"

"And developer, evidently. He wants to buy my lots at the lake."

"Why does he want those worthless lots?"

I felt offended. Maybe they weren't waterfront, but I thought they still had value. "I wouldn't call them worthless. The area has been picking up lately, with all the people from Kansas City buying up everything. Even Jack must think so. He offered me twice what I thought they were worth."

"Two times nothing is still nothing, Jake. If Morgan is interested in those lots, there must be a good reason." It was good to see her perk up. Her innate curiosity about Morgan's offer had made her forget her own problems. "Maybe," she added. Her eyes narrowed, and her posture stiffened. "He has insider information on finishing Highway 65."

"Why would that make the property more valuable?"

"Where have you been, Jake? Living under a rock? Haven't you heard the rumor that we might be chosen for the next lakeside resort? If they ever finish the four-lane highway to Springfield, we could be the next Big Cedar Lodge."

"No, I haven't heard the rumor, but it makes sense. We do have two of the largest lakes in the state, if not the country, and I suppose having a good road to get here would be a boon to developers."

Kelly must have had second thoughts. "However, that's not likely to happen anytime soon. It takes years to plan and approve a new highway, not to mention building it, but the rumor never seems to go away. I wonder why he wants those lots? It's not like him to..." Kelly's mouth fell open in the middle of her sentence and she stared at the front of the cafe. I turned to look at why she had suddenly stopped talking.

A middle-aged woman, wearing a business suit with a hair-do, straight out of Vogue, entered the cafe while the man she was with held the door open for her. He, too, was dressed up. I found it strange at first. The last time I'd worn a suit in this town was at a funeral, so I wondered who had died.

"That's Melissa Jacobs," Kelly said in a near whisper once she'd found her voice.

"Who?" I asked as the couple took a corner table near the back of the café away from everyone else.

She puckered her lips as though her cappuccino had fly larvae floating in it. "Our southside commissioner. She voted with Morgan to cut our budget. It's their fault I'm on traffic duty."

Melissa didn't notice us. Either she was preoccupied with the man at her table, or she failed to recognize Kelly.

They must have chosen the corner table to get some privacy because of its seclusion, allowing them to talk without anyone listening. Little did they realize the hard corner walls acted like an amphitheater, bouncing their conversation to our table. I couldn't help but hear them.

"This is important, Melissa, I need to convince you that your little town is the perfect spot for a casino. With two of the largest lakes in the state, it's the perfect spot for the next casino. Just think of what it will do for your local economy, not to mention the tax revenue it will bring in." His focus was on his companion as though they were the only ones in the room.

Melissa waved her hand as if she were swatting away his words. "I told you, I would think about it, Mark. Now let it go, would you? We don't even know if the house bill allowing them to build a casino on our lake will pass. Casinos are only allowed on the Missouri and Mississippi rivers."

The man, who I now knew as Mark, leaned back in his chair and put his hands behind his head. "Morgan says that's about to change. Both lakes feed the Missouri, so it should be a slam dunk. It is why he's scouting for locations. He needs to know we support him."

Mark might have thought his companion was the only one listening, but evidently, she didn't. She nodded her head toward the couple at the next table and lowered her voice. "I assume by 'support,' you mean incentive," she said so low I could barely hear her.

I could see Mark's reflection in the plate glass window. He had a malicious smile. "A little grease never hurt to get the wheels moving. Morgan has already started the lubrication with some of the lobbyists, now all we need is a shot of WD-40, if you know what I mean."

Melissa finished off the cappuccino she'd been sipping and got up. She was a lot less animated than she'd been a few minutes before. "Let me think about it, Mark. I need to sleep on it."

Mark got up, too, took her arm by the elbow, and led her out of the coffee shop. "Don't think too long. Opportunities like this don't come but once in a lifetime."

I looked around to see if anyone else was as startled by the conversation as I was. Most of the other customers had left before Mark hinted at Morgan's bribe. The couple at the table closest to them were too engrossed in themselves to pay Melissa and her friend any attention.

Fred had gone back to sleep at my feet but woke when the commissioners walked past our table. He put his head in my lap, looking for an ear scratch. "That explains why Morgan was so hot to buy my property," I said to Kelly while subconsciously giving Fred what he wanted.

"It also explains why he cut our budget," she said between clinched teeth.

"Look on the bright side, Kell. More tax dollars mean a bigger budget for the sheriff, which means he can hire a rookie to catch speeders and give you the job you deserve."

I was about to ask Kelly about the GSR test when our server brought coffee to our table. Fred sat up knowing all too well that the servers kept dog biscuits in their aprons.

"Is it all right if I give him a treat?" she asked, reaching into her apron after refilling my coffee. She kept her hand out of sight, but Fred knew she had a dog treat and he put his paw out.

"He's likely to follow you back to the kitchen if you don't," I said. Kelly had a small smile now. Maybe she was ready to tell me what was really bothering her.

"Is there something else you want to tell me?" I asked after the server gave Fred his treat and left.

Kelly's smile turned down again. "I should be happy; Mom has finally agreed to assisted living. It looks like I'm going to be a free woman soon." She was saying one thing but I could see she meant another. Her mother had been living with her ever since selling her home in Lee's Summit, which had put a huge damper on our relationship. Was she sad or conflicted about putting her mother in a home? I couldn't tell.

I reached across the table and took her hand in mine. "That's fantastic," I said. I wanted to add that she could move in with Fred and me, but I didn't want to press my luck.

She waited before speaking as though she had read my mind. Finally, she continued, "It also means I don't have to put up with nepotism. I've been thinking of applying to the Highway Patrol."

"Nepotism?" I asked, even though thoughts of her leaving town lingered in my mind.

"It's when someone promotes family over a better-qualified candidate."

"I know what nepotism is, Kell. Who did Bennett promote?"

She looked at me with cold, swollen eyes. "His nephew, Josh Teller. He made him a detective and put him in charge of Maddie's case, but not before declaring it a suicide. I think he was afraid I'd turn up something he didn't want uncovered."

She seemed to realize she'd said too much while looking around to see if anyone was listening. "Sorry if I sound bitter, Jake. I should be happy that Mom is finally moving somewhere she can get the care she needs. I'm afraid to leave her alone anymore. Just the other day, she'd left the stove burner on and almost started a fire. But enough of my problems. How is that new book of yours coming along?"

Fred had gone back to resting his head on his paws, so I knew he'd be no help for what I was about to ask. I fidgeted with the sleeve of my shirt while deciding how to ask her about the gunshot residue test without breeching a sore subject. "Well, when I was trying to come up with some kind of plot last night, I thought about Maddie."

She froze and her mouth dropped open. "I hope you don't use anything I said."

"I'm not. Or at least I'll change the names to protect the innocent." I could see she wasn't buying my little joke, or maybe she hadn't been raised on reruns of Dragnet as I had been. "Anyway, it occurred to me that if she did kill herself, there'd be gunshot residue on her hand, so I was wondering if you got the GSR results back from the coroner yet?"

She shook her head, making me wonder if I'd gone too far and crossed a line. Then she sighed. "It was positive, but I learned in one of the forensics classes I took that it can mean many things. It's not conclusive evidence that she pulled the trigger. Even the FBI no longer accepts it. They closed their GSR testing lab in 2006. But it was all Bennett needed to call it a suicide and close the case."

She had my imagination piqued. "Oh, are you saying it's not proof that she shot herself?"

Kelly's eyes seemed to turn inward, the way one does when they're thinking. "Someone could have forced her to hold the gun when they pulled the trigger, for one thing, or maybe shot her after killing her another way. There are many other ways to explain the GSR on her hand as well, but those are the most common."

"Won't an autopsy tell you if she was dead before being shot?"

She stared at me, as though I'd just told her there was no God. "It would, but Teller didn't order one. He said she died from the gunshot because of the amount of blood on the headboard."

"Yeah, I read somewhere that is indicative of a beating heart, which wouldn't happen if she was already dead." I didn't want to upset her any more than I already had and decided to change the subject as I reached out to hold her hand. "I imagine her husband was pretty upset when Bennett called him."

Her eyes narrowed until they were almost squinting. "Bennett didn't make the call. He had me do it." She paused and blinked slowly. "It was strange the way he reacted...or should I say, didn't react. He didn't show any emotion at all."

"Bonnie said they will probably divorce. Do you think it's possible her husband killed her and made it look like suicide?"

"Do you know something I don't, Jake?"

"No, I just meant it would have been a good locked-room murder to solve in my book."

"Don't you dare, Jake! You know how Bennett feels about you butting into our investigations." The hand I'd been caressing moments ago was now a clenched fist. Any hope I had about her moving in with me evaporated. Or so it seemed. Her outburst even startled Fred, waking him from whatever dream he was having.

"Sorry, Kell. It was just an idea for a book," I lied. "I promise I won't write anything that could get you in trouble."

Kelly groaned, and a small smile began to form on her lips. "And Bonnie? Something tells me you're not alone, and I'm not referring to your crime-solving canine. It seems Bonnie is always involved when you stick your nose where it doesn't belong."

"Bonnie, who?" I said before giving my Academy Award-winning fake laugh.

Chapter Five

FRED AND I HEADED for the lumber yard after leaving Fido's.
Bonnie had been after me to fix her front stairs as I couldn't
think of any good excuses to put off the task I'd started before
getting the calls from Jack Morgan and Kelly.

I couldn't shake the conversation I'd overheard between our
southside commissioner and her friend while picking out the
treated, two-by-ten boards Bonnie needed for her front porch
steps. There had been rumors about building a casino on our
part of the lake ever since I could remember. I'd even seen
several Facebook discussions about it, but they were just rumors. As Melissa Jacobs had told the well-dressed developer at
Fido's, the legislature would have to pass a new law before any
casinos could be built anywhere other than the Mississippi or
Missouri rivers. Maybe someone had found a way around the

law or a loophole. After all, Lake of the Ozarks used to feed the
Missouri which connects to the Mississippi before the dam in
Osage Beach was built during the Depression. It was called the
Osage River in those days and was a major riverboat route from
St. Louis to Western Missouri.

"We don't like people picking through the lumber. You have
to take what you need from the top." I had been so engrossed
in my thoughts, I failed to see the yardman come up behind
me and my lookout was off sniffing out another rack of lumber
where some critter must have been recently.

"Sorry, but some of these boards have more curves than a
pole dancer. I need them for stair treads, and they have to be
straight and knot-free."

The yardman crossed his arms and licked his lips. "I can't
make no exceptions, or we'd end up with a pile of firewood."

I felt like saying something about the noxious gasses released
when burning treated pine lumber for firewood, but I simply
nodded okay and called my worthless lookout. "Come on,
Fred, let's take what we've got and call it a day."

· · · ● · ● · · · ·

I couldn't stop thinking about the conversations at Fido's
while driving back to Bonnie's. It's funny how the mind
works. Instead of Melissa Jacobs's conversation with the de-

veloper, I found myself thinking about Kelly. It was obvious she wasn't happy that Bennett had promoted his nephew to detective over her, but was she really serious about leaving? My first thought was that I had to think of a way to make her change her mind, but that was being selfish. If she wanted to find a better job, it wasn't any of my business. Maybe I should think about moving to the KC area instead, assuming that was what she wanted. In a way, I hadn't lied to her at Fido's. Maddie's death did have me thinking about writing a locked-room murder. Didn't almost every famous mystery writer pen one of those novels? Okay, maybe I wasn't famous, but it was a better idea for a story than any other I could think of.

My first thought of having a hidden door in the room had been done so many times it was almost a cliche. Even variations of it, like trap doors in the floor and ceiling, were common. It got me to thinking if someone who had read too many mysteries might have used that as a way to murder Maddie. I had to find a way back into her house and check for hidden doors, but I had to do it without letting Kelly know.

Bonnie shoved her hands into her housecoat while watching me replace the rotted-out steps leading to her front porch. "Martha said that Maddie thought a casino would just bring in more crime and undesirables to the county."

I told her what Kelly and I had overheard at Fido's. Martha was one of Bonnie's quilting club friends. I think they met to gossip more than discuss quilting techniques.

She leaned back from her perch on the top step, nodding her approval of my work. "Rumor from the grapevine has it that she and Morgan were at each other's throats during the last commissioners' meeting. He's been buying up property near the lake as if the casino is a done deal, and if Maddie continued to oppose the deal, he'd be bankrupt."

"So, you think he killed her because she opposed any new development?"

"Or that guy at Fido's you told me about. It sounds like he and Morgan are up to something and trying to get the other commissioners to go along with it. Maddie was opposed to any new development, so that might be what got her killed."

"You are assuming she was murdered. The GSR test came back positive, and Bennet's new detective doesn't want to go against his uncle, who insists it's a suicide," I said as I screwed the last step into place.

Bonnie stood up and gave my work a thumbs-up with her right hand. "Those look like they'll last another hundred years, Jake. How about I fix us some lunch for all the hard work you did on them?" She didn't wait for me to respond before heading back into the house. Fred, who hadn't shown any interest in my handiwork and had been snoozing on the porch, woke up and followed her inside. I suppose that free meals were one of the advantages of living on her family's homestead. I couldn't remember the last time I had to feed myself or my dog.

• • • • •• • • • •

"I've been thinking, Jake," Bonnie said while refilling both of our cups. I had washed up and joined my team in her kitchen.

"Oh?" I said, taking my seat at the table and wondering what bombshell she was about to drop.

She hadn't moved from the table and was holding the coffee pot over my cup as if she'd forgotten she'd already filled it. "This whole thing with the GSR and Bennett being so quick to close the case doesn't smell right. On the other hand, if someone held the gun to Maddie's head with her hand on the trigger, they'd have to be pretty strong as she wasn't exactly a small woman. But there still is no way they could get out of that room unless there is a hidden door in the wall or something like that."

"That was my thought, too."

"I think we need to take a closer look at that room," she answered, returning the coffee pot to the kitchen counter.

"I agree, but how do we find a way into the house without breaking any laws or letting Kelly or Bennett know?" I snuck

Fred a piece of sausage under the table when she turned around to put the coffee pot back.

"I saw that, Jake. Have you forgotten I have eyes in the back of my head?" I'd forgotten she could see my reflection in her microwave's glass door.

I answered my own question before she could lecture me on feeding Fred people food. "You could pose as a potential buyer, but then the realtor would have to be there, and it would be difficult to search for a trap door."

Bonnie came back to the table, shaking her head. "Actually, that's not a bad idea, but instead of pretending to be a buyer, I think I have a better idea."

Chapter Six

YELLOW CRIME SCENE TAPE was still stretched across the front door when we went back to Maddie Summers' house. Bonnie's idea of pretending to be home inspectors seemed like a good idea at the time, but now I had my doubts. She had borrowed magnetic signs from a church friend of hers, whose son owned an inspection service, to put on the sides of her Jeep. I parked my truck so they could be seen by any passing vehicle or nosy neighbor.

"Do you think we should take down the tape?" she asked when we got to the front door.

I took a quick look up and down the road to see if anyone was watching, then carefully removed one end of the tape. "It's not a crime scene. Maddie killed herself, according to the sheriff. Remember, that's why we're here—to inspect the house for the listing agent," I said as I removed the screws holding the plywood Bennett's team had screwed over the door window I'd broken on our last visit.

Once I was able to reach in through the broken glass and turn the deadbolt, I opened the door and ushered Bonnie and Fred inside. It probably wasn't such a good idea to bring Fred with us, but I thought that Tigger must have followed a squirrel or was looking for mice when she got stuck in the bedroom with Maddie's corpse, so Fred would be able to sniff out a hidden door better than either of us, especially if any rodents had made a home in the walls.

Bonnie went straight for the bedroom while I decided to measure the adjacent walls. If there was a hidden hallway in one of the walls, it would have to be wider than the normal four or five inches of a regular stud wall with drywall on each side, or in the case of old houses like this, lath and plaster were used long before drywall was invented.

When I didn't see any anomalies in the walls, I decided I'd check to see if Bonnie had found anything.

"Don't let Fred near those dead bugs; they're disgusting," she said when I entered the room.

As if on cue, Fred went over to a vent by the highboy and sniffed a bunch of dead cockroaches. "No, Fred!" I yelled before he decided to taste them.

He listened to me for once and backed away with his tail between his legs.

I turned to Bonnie to explain why I yelled. "Maddie probably sprayed around the vents before meeting her maker. Those bugs would be like poison to a dog. She couldn't run the furnace without power. Either that or it must have run out of propane some time ago for there to be so many bugs in the ducts," I said, petting Fred on the head to let him know I wasn't mad at him.

Bonnie refused to look at the bugs. "Probably afraid they'd get to her after she died. That's something I'd worry about if I knew I'd be stuck dead in a room with bugs, so maybe she did kill herself."

I looked around for a can of bug spray but couldn't see one. "I'll check out under the sink while you look for trap doors."

Bonnie blinked and spoke in a softer voice, "Why would she go to the trouble of putting the can back under the sink if she planned on shooting herself?" Her tone suggested she was thinking out loud, not asking me a question.

"Some habits are hard to break, and while you're checking for a way out, don't bother looking for a hidden passage in the wall next to the hall. It's barely six inches thick."

"Maybe it was the Thin Man," Bonnie said with a giggle.

I didn't crack a smile.

"It's a joke, Jake. Loosen up."

"I was thinking, Bon."

She started to say something, then stopped as though she had second thoughts. "Oh, so you think it was somebody really thin?"

"No. A thought had entered my mind, and I couldn't let it go. If Tigger found her way into the bedroom, why didn't she leave the same way she came in?"

Bonnie looked at me blankly. She was no longer smiling. "You don't suppose she came in before Maddie did herself in and got trapped when she blocked the door?"

"That, or the killer didn't see Tigger. Either way, let's keep looking for a hidden door."

• • • • • • • • • •

The house had been built at a time when open kitchens weren't in any of the design magazines, assuming those periodicals existed back then. The rooms were small and compartmentalized, with the kitchen and stairs leading to the basement at the back of the house. Fred had gone on ahead of me and was sniffing at the door to the basement when I entered the kitchen.

"What's up, old boy? Is there something down there?" I opened the door, and he ran down the stairs without answering me.

"The bedroom is clear." I jerked my head back and felt my blood pressure jump.

"Bonnie! You surprised me."

"Is that a basement? Oh, I get it. You're going down there to see if there's a trap door the murderer used, aren't you?"

"Unless you have a better idea. Fred is already down there, but I doubt if he's looking for trap doors."

Bonnie nodded, then grinned. "Knowing Freddie, he must have smelled something to eat."

I turned from Bonnie, fished my cellphone out of my pocket, and turned on its flashlight.

Bonnie peeked down the stairs. "It looks like you have to pull on that string hanging from the light bulb at the bottom of the stairs. Of course, that's not going to help with the power out."

"These old houses had the electric panel in the basement so, with a little luck, I'll be able to get us some light. Let's hope the bulb isn't burned out if I do get the power back on," I said, starting down. I'd thought about saying something about how, in the movies, there is always a deranged killer waiting for his victim and for Bonnie to run out and call for help if she hears me scream but thought better of it. I knew those things only happened in the movies but did Bonnie?

I found the panel on the far wall and was surprised to see it had been upgraded with a main breaker. I flipped the breaker, and the light at the bottom of the stairs went on. When I didn't get knocked over the head by an ax murderer, I called up for Bonnie to join me. We started on the wall nearest the stairs and continued around the perimeter checking for outside entrances. It wasn't a tall basement. The exposed floor joists were only an inch or two above my head, causing me to duck when we came to the main beam supporting the joists. The walls were made of chiseled rocks cemented together with mortar that had long ago turned back to sand. I assumed the original builders had gathered the foundation stones from the property. It was a common practice a hundred years ago, but it wouldn't pass modern building codes. Only the weight of the rocks was stopping the foundation from falling down. Then I examined each window lock. They hadn't been opened in years and even if they had, they were all too small for anything other than a cat to climb through, let alone a grown man. There was nothing that looked like an exit.

"If I've got my bearings right, we must be under her bedroom. I don't see anything that looks like a trapdoor--do you?" I said once we'd finished our inspection of the walls, and I was checking out the floor joists by shining my phone's light at them. They looked to be about sixteen inches on center so if there was a trap door between them, it would have to be very narrow.

Bonnie let out her breath in a sigh. " I didn't find anything in the bedroom to suggest one."

"Did you check the ceiling?" I asked.

"Of course, I did, and the walls by tapping on them for any voids. I read murder mysteries, too, you know. However, you may want to check out the closet. I didn't bother in there because there were boxes stacked against the wall and they didn't look like they had been moved in ages. If it has a false wall, it would have been impossible for anyone to stack those boxes against it after leaving the room."

"Hmm...what about attic access? Did you see that in there? They usually put those in closets."

Fred started barking from upstairs before Bonnie could answer. It sounded like he was at the front door.

"I don't remember him going back up the stairs. Did he pass you on your way down?"

Bonnie raised her eyebrows and shrugged. "No. I thought he was down here with you. How did he get past us?"

I thought about checking for an outside entrance again in case we'd missed it on our first inspection, but we had probably been too occupied to notice him going back upstairs. Besides, I knew Fred's bark. He must be warning us that someone was either coming down the drive or up the porch stairs. "Hold on, Fred. I'm coming," I said and handed the phone to Bonnie. "I'll see what's going on. Why don't you take a closer look to see if we missed an outside entrance? These old houses sometimes have cellar doors on the outside, and the stairway might be hidden by boxes or something."

· • • •• • • •• · ·

"Shouldn't he be on a leash before he bites someone?" A middle-aged man with a comb-over that failed to cover his balding scalp was standing on the first step of the porch, holding up his right hand to fend off Fred. I hadn't recognized him without his John Deere hat, but the voice was unforgettable. "He won't bite you unless I tell him to, Jack," I said, grabbing Fred's collar in case he proved me wrong. "What can I do for you?" I should have told him the worst Fred would do is lick him to death, but his abrasive attitude rekindled my dislike toward him.

He began swaying from side to side, and his eyes narrowed. "You can start by telling me what you're doing at a crime scene."

He now had me on the defensive, and I couldn't quite look him in the eyes. "It's not a crime scene, Jack. Bennett is sure Maddie killed herself, so he closed the case. I'm here to inspect the property for the real estate firm representing the family. I'm afraid I can't let you in until we're done."

"We?" he asked, scratching his jaw.

I could feel my voice rise and seriously thought about letting go of Fred's collar. "Fred and me. You know, Fred, my dog?" I realized there was no sense in mentioning Bonnie and possibly getting her into trouble. I was already facing arrest if the man didn't buy my story. Bonnie didn't need that.

Morgan relaxed as a smile began to form on his face. "Who is it, Jake?" Bonnie asked. I hadn't heard her come up behind me.

"Good morning, Mrs. Jones." His expression turned wicked. "I see you are up to your old tricks again."

"What are you doing here, Morgan?" She didn't sound happy to see him.

"I don't see how that's any of your business, but if you must know, I was driving by when I saw Jake's truck parked in the driveway. I didn't know he was in the inspection business, so I thought I'd ask how much work needs to be done to the old firetrap before making an offer on it. When did you go into the business, Mrs. Jones?"

I saw Bonnie's reflection in Morgan's glasses. Her mouth had dropped wide enough for a small bird to fly in. "I haven't. I'm helping Jake. It's his business, and the house isn't on the market yet."

"Just the way I like them," he said, and stepped up to the porch next to Bonnie. Then before either of us could react, he walked into the house.

All three of us followed Morgan as he walked through the living room. Bonnie calmed down by the time we'd made the short trip to the bedroom. Morgan went straight to the tallboy dresser that some of the deputies had put back upright.

"No worse for wear," he said as he ran his hand over the worn patina. I heard she tipped it over to block the door before shooting herself."

"I didn't know that information was common knowledge." Bonnie had her hands on her hips, and by the look on her face, she was no longer intimidated by the man.

Morgan crossed his arms and inhaled deeply. I could see the veins in his neck expand. "What--the fact that she shot herself or she blocked the door?"

"The latter," I said. "Who told you she tipped over the tallboy?"

Morgan smiled and looked at the dresser, now standing upright. "So, that's what you call those monstrosities?"

Bonnie rolled her eyes. "Yes, and some are quite valuable."

Morgan suddenly became interested in antique furniture. "Oh? I was going to ask Maddie's daughter to sell the house to me furnished without the expense of listing it, but I guess I'm too late if Gloria already has the listing. Guess I'll have to ask her."

I'd forgotten about Gloria's for sale sign outside and wondered if Jack would find out we weren't real inspectors and had no right to be here. I saw a flush break out on Bonnie's neck and jumped in before she could perjure us any further.

"We were hired by the estate lawyer so I doubt if Gloria knows about the inspection."

"I thought you said you were hired by the listing agent. Maybe I'd better call Maddie's daughter then," he said, looking at me. It was more of a smirk as if he'd just beaten me at poker. His upper lip seemed to curl up before he turned his back to us and walked toward the door. He turned just before leaving the bedroom. "And by the way, Jake, I'll hold off saying anything to the sheriff about you two pretending to be home inspectors for now. It might be a bit inconvenient for you to sell your property to me if you're sitting in a jail cell."

"Did he just blackmail you?" Bonnie asked as I let Fred go. I almost hoped he would go after Morgan and bite him in the rear, but he must have felt my mood change, and sat next to me, pushing his big snout into my dangling hand.

"That obvious, huh?"

Chapter Seven

KELLY STARTED TO REPLY, then closed her mouth. It was obvious she was looking for the right words. "I'll have to tell Bennett, you know." We were sitting at her kitchen table taking a break from moving her mother into assisted living. I had loaded some of the heavier boxes in a U-Haul van Kelly had rented and I had just finished telling her how Bonnie and I had posed as home inspectors as an excuse to search for trap doors in Maddie's bedroom.

"Yeah, I know. I thought maybe you could say something like I misunderstood you and thought I was doing you a favor by confirming there were no hidden doors in the bedroom."

Her eyes turned cold, and her face reddened. "Jake!"

I swallowed for the third time in as many minutes and forced myself to look her in the eyes. "Maybe you can say Fred found a way into the house and couldn't get back out, so we had to break in to rescue him."

"What part of 'don't butt into the investigation' don't you understand, Jake?"

"I didn't think there was an investigation. Bennett said Maddie killed herself, and the case was closed. "

Kelly tried not to smile, and I knew her anger had been an act. "Don't blame it on Freddie just because he's not here to defend himself."

"Tigger would be more believable." It was Kelly's mom who had spoken, startling us both. "You could say she got in through the chimney or an open window and couldn't get back out."

"Mom! How long have you been standing there eavesdropping?"

"Long enough to watch you on your high horse. How can you not help the man who saved your job more times than I can count?"

Mrs. Brown let go of her walker and stood straight, waving a finger at her daughter. "I can't believe you'd put poor Jake in jail and let that nasty realtor get away with murder. Who's going to take care of his dog? By the way, where is Freddie?"

Kelly's smile vanished as she turned to face her mother. "Your new home doesn't allow pets, so Jake left him at Bonnie's, and for the record, I wouldn't let Jake go to jail. I just wanted to make him squirm a little. I would have thought of something to tell Bennett."

Mrs. Brown walked slowly to the table and sat down on the nearest chair. "Well, honey, why don't you get your mother a cup of tea while I ask Jake about this blackmailer?"

She leaned forward in her chair while her daughter made her tea. Her short, white hair and missing bottom denture reminded me so much of my own mother. "Tell me, Jake. What made you go back into that house anyway? Kelly told me that Maddie shot herself, and the sheriff considers it a suicide. Do you think otherwise?"

"Bonnie is convinced Maddie didn't kill herself, and the enigma of a locked room murder was too much for my imagination. I just had to check and see if there was a hidden door in the walls or floor that a murderer could have used after shooting Maddie."

"I think I understand your curiosity. I've read all of your books, and I think I understand how that mind of yours works. I also know Bonnie, or at least I know how she thinks--she isn't that much younger than me. And that dog of yours has helped you solve several murders, even if they were fiction, but why does she think Maddie didn't shoot herself? Kelly told me they found gunshot residue on her hands. Isn't that proof she shot herself?"

Kelly rolled her eyes; she had joined us at the table and passed a cup of tea to her mother. "I told you, Mom, GSR isn't conclusive evidence. Someone could have made her hold the gun as they pulled the trigger, and the murders Fred help solve weren't fiction, Mom."

Mrs. Brown swatted the air at an imaginary fly. "I'm not senile you know. Of course, I remember. I just wanted to see what Jake had to say, and I hope it's the real stuff and not that decaf crap you try to pawn off on me."

"It's real, Mom. I made it only five minutes ago, so it's still fresh, too."

"Did you put sugar and cream in it? You know I like my tea with two sugars and a bit of cream; not enough to ruin it, but just enough to color it." She'd said it for my benefit, I'm sure, as Kelly didn't need to be reminded of her mother's preferences.

Mrs. Brown took a sip of the brew and made a sour face before setting it down on the table in front of her. She continued without commenting on the tea. "So, what made Bonnie think our esteemed commissioner didn't kill herself? By the way, I've really got to meet her. She seems a lot like me."

"She's dead, Mom. Unless you want me to take you to the morgue, I don't think it's possible to meet her."

It was Mrs. Brown's turn to roll her eyes. "Bonnie, Missy, not the dead woman." She picked up her tea and took a sip without making any faces.

I saw my chance to get a word in before mother and daughter forgot the question. "Her daughter is expecting. Bonnie says it was all she talked about, being a grandmother for the first time. Does that sound like a woman who would kill herself?"

Both women turned toward me as though I were a burning bush. Mrs. Brown was the first to respond. "No, it doesn't. Not that I'd ever know what it's like being a grandmother," she added, giving her daughter a cold stare.

Kelly blushed and lowered her eyes. "Well, it's out of my hands now." She looked up at me. "I've got an interview with the Highway Patrol next week."

Kelly's mother sighed, slowly shaking her head. "The Highway Patrol? You could be put anywhere in the state. I was hoping to see you at least once a week. What if they put you in Jefferson City or somewhere down south? I'll never see you."

"They need officers in the Kansas City area, too. If I get one of those openings, I'll see you every day," Kelly said after going over to hug her mother and wipe the tears away from her eyes. "You know I wouldn't leave you all alone, don't you?"

· · · · ●·●· · ·

I left mother and daughter alone to finish packing and drove back home. There was a sheriff's truck parked in Bonnie's driveway when I pulled in, and I knew it wasn't Kelly.

Chapter Eight

FRED WAS WAITING FOR me at the door when I let myself into the house. He acted as if I'd been gone for months. He kept running back and forth, brushing up against me. "Is everything okay, Bon?" I yelled when I didn't see her or the deputy.

"We're in the kitchen, Jake," she answered.

Deputy Charlie Browne was standing at Bonnie's kitchen counter. I knew him from when he'd done some forensics last year during another murder investigation. People always kidded him about his last name or thought he was related to Kelly. She was the first to point out that hers didn't have an 'e' at the end. We called him Deputy Charlie to avoid confusion with both Kelly and the cartoon character.

I didn't recognize his partner, however. This guy was busy writing in a notebook while sitting at the kitchen table. Unlike the clean-cut Deputy Charlie, this deputy sported the unshaven face of someone who was trying to grow a beard. That, along with an overdue haircut, made him look more like a criminal than a cop. He stopped writing and looked up at me when Fred and I entered the kitchen.

"You must be the infamous Jake Martin, and I take it your companion there is Fred?" His expression was pinched, like someone who had a bad headache.

"And you are?" I asked while glancing over at Bonnie, who was sitting at the far side of the table. It looked as if she were about to say something but then had second thoughts and closed her mouth.

"Detective Teller. I've been assigned to tie up some loose ends in the suicide of Madeline Summers. I think you know my deputy already," he said, nodding at Charlie.

I acknowledged Charlie with a head gesture, "I thought you quit last year."

Charlie wouldn't look me in the eyes as he replied. "The new job wasn't what I thought it was, and Bennett offered me my old job back."

I'd heard he had quit when he followed a fellow officer, Deputy Johnson, to the sheriff's department in Clinton, it was something I'd have to ask Kelly about later, and turned my attention back to Teller. "How can you be sure she killed herself? Just because the GSR test came back positive doesn't mean someone else couldn't have staged the shooting."

"How do you know the results of the test?" His eyes narrowed as he tried to stare me down.

"I think I read it online somewhere. Her suicide is a hot topic in all the local newsgroups."

His posture stiffened as he laughed sarcastically. "Yeah, right. Anyway, I need to ask you where you were last night before you two have a chance to make alibis for each other," he said, shrugging his head in Bonnie's direction.

"Are you okay, Bonnie?" I asked, ignoring Teller.

"Someone killed Morgan last night, Jake. And dummkopf here thinks we had something to do with it."

Teller held up a hand toward Bonnie. I could see the whites of his eyes as he glared at me. "Witnesses saw him arguing with you at your lake property last week and again yesterday at the house where Mrs. Summers died. They said it looked like you were ready to hit him. Now, are you going to tell me where you were last night and what you were doing at the house where Mrs. Summers died, or do you want to tell Sheriff Bennett at the station?"

"I told you; he was here until eight having dinner with me," Bonnie said. She was now standing, ready to take on the deputy even though she was a good foot shorter and thirty years older than him.

"Sit down, old lady. I said I wanted to hear his alibi without you covering for him. You think I don't know you two are in this together?" Teller was nearly shouting, and had his hand on the butt of his stun gun. Luckily, Bonnie realized his anger and backed off, sitting down in her chair.

Fred was baring his teeth and trying to get out of his collar. I tightened my grip and pushed him farther behind me when I saw Teller's hand move from his stun gun to the pepper spray can on his belt. "No need to get riled up, Detective. I ate dinner here, then went home to work on my latest novel."

"And what did you have for dinner?" The detective's Adam's apple bulged as he swallowed. I could only hope it was rage and not a heart attack.

"Pot roast, boiled potatoes, and broccoli. I passed on the broccoli, though. Then we had apple pie for dessert. Bonnie even gave Fred some of the pot roast but no broccoli. He's like me and thinks that only wimps eat broccoli," I tried to diffuse the situation by making a joke, but the detective wasn't amused.

"Well, you're either telling the truth, or you guys rehearsed this before. And why were you at the old lady's house who killed herself?"

"Research for my book. I wanted to check out the room where she died. Details are everything in a murder mystery."

Teller scratched at his three-day beard. "It's no mystery. She shot herself. Anyway, I'll let the sheriff know your alibis check out. At least, for now."

Fred finally stopped growling after Teller and Charlie left. He had to have the last word, though and barked at the officers just before they got into their truck.

I was on the phone with Kelly before Teller and Charlie were out of the drive. "Hi, Kell. How's everything at your mom's new home?"

"It took some time to get her settled in. I sure hope I'm doing the right thing, but why is a little birdie telling me that's not why you called?"

"Teller and his shadow were just here."

"Charlie?"

"Yep, Deputy Fife is back."

The pause on the other end of the line meant Kelly didn't know what to say, or she'd dropped her phone. "What did they want?" she asked after the pause.

"It looks like someone killed Morgan, and Teller wanted to check my alibi. I don't understand why he thinks I did it. I barely knew the man."

"Stay where you are, Jake. I'll be right over. I'm almost in Truman now."

· · · • • · • • · ·

"Morgan's dead?" I asked once I'd gone back to Bonnie's kitchen and poured myself a cup of coffee from the pot on her counter that always seemed to be on.

She blinked slowly and looked at me with her tired, gray eyes. "That's what he said. So, does this mean we're back to square one on who killed Maddie?"

"Looks like it, but don't tell Kelly we're snooping around. She should be here shortly," I answered.

Chapter Nine

SOMETHING WAS WRONG. KELLY'S hug felt like I was embracing a lifeless mannequin. "Is your mom okay?" I asked after I released her.

Fred felt it, too. He didn't try to stick his snout in her hand the way he usually does when he hasn't seen her in fifteen minutes. He sat by my side with his ears back and head down.

"Six years I've given him, and what do I have to show for it?" I could see her eyes were red from crying, something I hadn't noticed before trying to greet her with our usual embrace.

"I take it you're talking about the sheriff?" Bonnie asked once Kelly sat down on the living room sofa. Bonnie had taken a seat in one of her matching Queen Anne chairs directly across from Kelly, leaving the sofa for me to sit next to Kelly. I could tell Kelly might have gotten up and left if I did that, so I took a seat in the other matching chair. Fred laid down by my feet and put his head on his paws, but kept an eye on Kelly. I knew he was waiting for a signal from her to come over so she could rub his head, but it never came.

Her head was down, looking at her hands resting in her lap. "That case should be mine. I really thought Bennett was better than that. God, I hope I get that job with the Highway Patrol."

I felt so bad for her that I got up from my chair to sit next to her. "I'm sorry, Kell, but you always have us," I said, putting my arm around her shoulder. Fred had managed to squeeze in between our feet. It was too much for Kelly to ignore, she could no longer hold back her tears.

"I think we all need a shot of fortified coffee," Bonnie said as she got up to go to her kitchen. I knew she wasn't talking about adding hazelnut flavoring but didn't say anything. Kelly looked like she could use something stronger, even if I didn't.

· · · · ●·●·●· ·

After several cups of Bonnie's brew, Kelly began to loosen up and tell us about Teller. "Bennett claims he promoted him to lead detective because he had homicide experience from when he worked in Kansas City." The hard edge to her voice told us she wasn't buying it. "But we both know blood is thicker than water."

I could see Bennett's reasoning, despite Teller being his sister's son. Except for cooking meth, shootings over an unfaithful spouse, or an occasional argument over the neighbor's dog, kids, or property line, Fremont County didn't have a lot of crime. We didn't have anywhere near the homicides that Kansas City did, and I could see why he thought Josh was better qualified for the job. However, it wasn't something I wanted to share with Kelly at the moment.

"Martha says he was fired from his job in the city," Bonnie said from the comfort of her Queen Anne.

Kelly's facial muscles went slack. "That's the first I've heard about him being fired," she said. "Did Martha say why he was fired?"

Bonnie leaned back in her chair and seemed to be reveling in the gossip. "No. It was all hush-hush, from what I hear."

As intriguing as Bonnie's gossip was, I needed to make Kelly feel better rather than pour gasoline on her fire. "Well, whatever the reason for his promotion, I think he needs to show Bennett what he can do, and unfortunately, he will have no qualms about throwing Bonnie and me under the bus in his search for Morgan's killer."

"Do you suppose the same person killed them both?" Bonnie said. She finished her coffee and was about to get a refill.

Her question had been addressed to Kelly and not me, but I answered anyway. "That's a possibility. I could have sworn

Maddie killed herself, but now I wonder if someone isn't killing off our county's commissioners and why. We didn't see any trap doors or false walls in Maddie's bedroom for someone to leave after killing her, but maybe we missed something."

Kelly's eyebrows raised several inches. "You didn't tell him you were snooping around Maddie's, did you?" I was waiting for her to say something about interference from Bonnie and me as a major reason she didn't get the promotion, but if she had thought that, she never mentioned it.

"No, I'm not stupid. He already knew. Someone reported me arguing with Morgan at Maddie's just before he left. Its why Teller wanted to question me."

Kelly straightened up and scratched her chin. "There isn't a neighbor anywhere near that place. I wonder who saw you two arguing."

"I've been wondering about that, too. If it had been someone driving by, we should have seen them but regardless, I guess I'm the main suspect in Morgan's murder. Teller would probably like to pin Maddie's murder on me, too, but he's too dense to accept that she didn't kill herself."

"He's going to need more than an anonymous witness who saw you two arguing to do that, or is there something you're not telling me?"

I sipped on my coffee, hot and black the way I liked it, and sighed. "I thought I told you, he wanted to buy my property, and when I said I'd think about it, he went ballistic. He even threatened to pull strings with the health department so I wouldn't be able to get a septic permit."

"That's it?" she asked, shaking her head. I could almost see the wheels turning behind her red eyes. "That doesn't sound like much of a motive to kill someone."

"I didn't kill anyone, Kell. Just ask Fred; he was there."

She opened her mouth to speak, then paused as if collecting her thoughts. "I know that, and you would think Bennett would, too, after all the murder cases you helped him close," she said after finding the right words.

"Ungrateful is what he is if you ask me." Bonnie had taken it upon herself to refill Kelly's cup and add a little more of her fortification to it.

Kelly waved her off. "I've got to get back to my mother. The new home has her upset and I need to be there for her. If I drink any more of your coffee, I won't be driving anywhere."

· · ● · ● · ● ● · ·

After giving Kelly a peck on the cheek and watching her go down the driveway, I looked at my dog, "I think her job means more to her than we do, Freddie," I said, recalling how she'd flinched when I tried to hug her and tell her it would be okay.

This wasn't the first time I'd been a suspect in a murder. I've managed to clear my name before by finding the real culprit and it was obvious I'd have to do the same now. But where should I start? I suppose that finding out who saw me arguing with Morgan should be my first step. We'd argued twice. Once at my lake property and again at Maddie's house. Was it the same person who claimed to see us both times? That didn't make sense. Maddie's house was nowhere in sight of any of her neighbors, so how could someone have seen us unless they were watching with binoculars? I'd have to ask Kelly who had made the anonymous reports, but that would have to wait. I'd deal with Kelly after she got her mother settled.

· · · · ● · ● · · · ·

There was a text from Kelly the next morning. She apologized for being short with me the day before and said she got a copy of Teller's report and asked to meet me at Fred's favorite coffee shop. She guaranteed it would make my day. I could only hope the report mentioned the anonymous tipster.

Chapter Ten

FRED AND I WERE sitting in Fido's, waiting for Kelly to show when I got another text. Something came up, she said she couldn't make it, but sent me a copy of Teller's report and another of Maddie's suicide text. Maddie had supposedly sent it to her sister on the night of her death. It must have been what Kelly was so excited about. The text was short and to the point, and as with most texts, without punctuation: "Julia please forgive me for taking Morgan's money I did it for you and the kids but now that it's going public, I can't face the humiliation. I have nothing left to live for Maddie."

The text implied that Maddie killed herself because of a bribe she'd taken from Morgan. I suppose it was all Teller needed to put the case to rest. His report didn't mention who claimed to have seen me arguing with Morgan.

I answered Kelly's text with one of my own: "Something isn't right. Why didn't she send that text to Stephanie, too? Maddie didn't need money. The fee she was receiving for leasing her land was enough to support a small nation. Besides, she was against development. Why would she take a bribe?" Unlike most people, I took care to use punctuation and capitalization.

"Can't talk now." was her reply. Kelly didn't like to type. She used voice to text when she sent a message, which meant she could have talked if she wanted to. I'd have to wait to get her answer.

"Jake? Jake Martin?" An older woman who looked vaguely familiar had just picked up her coffee and was on her way to sit down when she saw me sitting at my table. "I wasn't sure it was you, then I saw Fred," she said sitting down across from me.

"Guilty as charged," I answered, racking my brain trying to put a name to her face. She had to be pushing seventy, so either I'd seen her at one of Bonnie's gossip sessions that she called luncheons or maybe at her church. I often joined Bonnie at church and then for coffee and doughnuts after the Sunday service.

She reached into the purse she had plopped on the table while still talking. "I've been carrying this book around, hoping I'd run into you," she said, rummaging through her bag. The purse was closer to the size of a small suitcase than a handbag. It made me think of my own mother's purse. She used to carry everything in it. She was more prepared for disaster than a Boy Scout den mother.

I suddenly remembered where I'd seen the woman. She had asked a million questions the last time I'd had a book signing at the local library. However, I still didn't know her name. "I hope you don't mind signing it for me," she said after producing a tattered paperback copy of my first novel.

"Not at all. I'd be more than happy to. Is there anything you'd like me to say?" I didn't want to hurt her feeling by asking for a name, so I hoped my subterfuge worked.

She leaned forward and lightly touched my arm. "To Rose, my biggest fan, would be nice." Her thick glasses did nothing to hide the excitement I saw in her cloudy brown eyes.

"To Rose, my biggest fan," I wrote then slid the book across the table. "I'm flattered you remember me. It's been a couple of years since I did the signing at the library, Rose."

She sat back, laying a hand over her heart. "Who could forget Truman's greatest private detective? I'll bet you and Bonnie are working on the commissioners' murders, aren't you?"

Now, I knew where I'd heard her name. She must be the Rose that Bonnie said told her about the sheriff and Maddie having an affair. I needed to be careful of what I said or it might get back to Kelly.

I winked, pretending to play along, and said in a whisper, "Don't let anyone know, but between you and me, I don't think it was suicide either."

"I wish I could be a fly on the wall when you ask Maddie's sister about the phony text," she said, her eyes sparkling through her thick lenses.

I felt my eyebrows rise. "You know about the text?"

"Of course, doesn't everyone?"

Fred pushed his wet nose against my leg, letting me know he had business to take care of, so I cut the conversation short. "I'll be sure to mention your help, Rose, if I ever write about it," I said, heading for the door before Fred decided to do his business on the table leg.

Something about the text Maddie had sent her sister bothered me, too. Then I realized what it was. I couldn't get service at Maddie's house when I tried to call 911, so how did she manage? I needed to talk to Maddie's sister about it. "So, I'm not the only one who thinks the text might be phony," I said to Fred as he watered the closest bush. "Any idea how we can find this Julia whatever her last name is without asking Kelly?"

Fred pointed his nose toward the buildings down the street and barked. My eyes looked in the direction he was pointing, but I didn't see what he was barking at. It was probably a cat or another dog. There was no way he could have understood my question, let alone tried to answer it, but I decided to walk down the sidewalk anyway.

The sheriff must have Julia's address and contact information, but I didn't want to ask Kelly for it unless I absolutely had to. The thought that I could do an Internet search of Maddie's social media to see if she talked to her daughter on Facebook or Instagram came to me while walking down the street, but the chances of her making that public was slim. She had been a prominent public servant whose private life could be exploited if she were careless. Even her friend list was probably blocked from prying eyes. Then it hit me when I noticed the funeral home across the street. Obituaries would list her family members, living or dead.

Fred saw the light go on in my head, and he looked up at me, smiling.

I really had to get a grip on reality if I thought that was what Fred was trying to tell me outside the coffee shop, but I played along anyway. "Good boy, Freddie."

Asking someone inside the funeral home would be the fastest, if not the easiest, way to get the information I needed, but I didn't want to leave a trace of my search just yet. It might get back to Teller and get Kelly in trouble if he thought I was snooping into his case. I suppose Maddie's obituary would be in the paper, but that only came out once a week. I didn't want to wait another four days for it to be published. Thank, God, for the Internet, I thought.

Fred had been waiting for me to follow up on my earlier praise, so I patted him on the head. "Come on, Fred--let's head home to do some online sleuthing."

· · · · ●·● ● · · ·

I found more than I was looking for within fifteen minutes of starting my search. The local funeral home did, indeed, have an online obituary for Madeline Summers. It said that she was survived by a daughter, Stephanie Travers of Clinton, Missouri, a sister, Julia Reston of Arvada, Colorado; and a husband, Michael Summers. Sadly, another daughter was listed under deceased relatives, as were a brother, father, mother, and grandparents.

My last search found Julia Reston's phone number in Arvada. It was only seven o'clock in Colorado, so I decided to call the sister, hoping she could confirm the suicide text. I just needed a way to ask without raising any eyebrows.

"Mrs. Reston?" I said after someone answered on my fourth ring.

"If this is a telemarketer, we don't need an automobile warranty, medical insurance, or to answer any surveys; otherwise

leave a message. I may or may not call you back." The someone
was voicemail.

"Mrs. Reston, my name is Jake Martin. I'm calling in regards
to your sister, Madeline Summers. I was the one who found
her, and I just wanted to say how sorry I am for your loss. I
was hoping I could talk to you about something she did just
before...well before she passed. Please call me back whenever
you can." I gave her my number in case she didn't have caller
ID and hung up.

She called back almost immediately, and I answered without
letting it go to voice mail. "Jake Martin?"

"Thank you for calling back, Mrs. Reston. I hope I didn't
catch you at a bad time."

"No, and please call me Julia. Tell me, are you the author
Maddie was always talking about? The one who solves crimes
in her county with his golden retriever and seventy-year-old
neighbor?"

"I'm flattered your sister knew about me."

"I don't think she ever read any of your books, but she did
talk about how you solved more murders down there than the
local police. She had a lot of respect for you and your neighbor.
Is that why you're calling me? You don't believe she killed
herself either, do you?"

"I don't know what to believe, but from what I saw, I don't
see how anyone could have shot her and got out of the room.

The only exit was blocked by a dresser from the inside. Did she sound depressed or down to you?"

"A little but I doubt if it was anything to cause her to kill herself."

"Oh? What had her down?" Maybe she had done herself in. I didn't want to make Maddie's sister feel any worse, but now I had to know.

"The last time I heard from her, I guess it was the night she died, she said that she was feeling bad about putting her daughter up for adoption after her twin died, but she was overjoyed that Stephanie was having a baby. She couldn't wait to be a grandmother."

"Maddie had twins?"

"Ashley and Amber. Ashley died in a house fire. I remember it was Halloween. I think 1980. I'm not sure, it's been so long. She was depressed, and put Amber up for adoption shortly after. I think she blamed her for her sister's death."

My mouth fell open. It took me a few seconds to recover, "Are you still there, Jake?" Julia asked.

"Sorry. My dog knocked the phone out of my hand," I lied.

"So, she didn't text you the night she died?" I asked after remembering my main reason for the call.

"Of course not. She hated texting. She always called. The last time was the day before."

It was a good thing Julia couldn't see my mouth fall open again. She just confirmed what Rose had said, that the text was phony. "Well, I just wanted to let you know that I'm here if you need anything and how sorry I am."

"I appreciate that, Jake, but knowing your reputation, I think you had other reasons for calling me. I hope you prove she didn't kill herself. We are Catholic, and you would be doing me a great favor if you could prove she didn't kill herself."

I didn't want to give her any false hope, but I'd been raised a Catholic myself, and I knew they believed suicide was a mortal sin. "I'm sure God knows the truth. He will welcome her even if we can't prove otherwise."

There was a pause on the other end. Her voice was trembling when she came back on. "Thank you, Jake."

"My other phone is ringing," I lied again. "Please take care, Julia," I said, disconnecting the call. I didn't know whether I should be pleased with myself for proving that Madeline hadn't sent the text or ashamed that I'd upset her sister.

So, the suicide text was phony. Had Teller fabricated it, or had someone else put it on her phone? Whoever it was had probably killed her, too.

I might have gone on searching for more information on Maddie and her daughters all night if I hadn't been interrupted by a text from Kelly. "Jake, sorry I can't call right now, but Mom burned herself cooking dinner. The home called me. I'm on my way to the ER in Lee's Summit. I'll keep you updated. Luv, Kell." Her text included an emoji of a broken heart.

I texted back that I loved her, too, and asked if she needed me to drive up to the ER. She responded that she had it under control, and I'd just be in the way. There was no emoji this time.

Fred had no idea what the text was about or what a text was, for that matter, while he continued to sleep at my feet. Sometimes, I envied him.

It was too late to work on my book, even if I wanted to, so I shut off my computer and headed for bed. I tried not to wake him, but I couldn't move my legs without bumping into his big head.

He simply raised his head to see what I was doing, and went back to sleep once I left the room. There was a time when any sudden movement would have made him jump up with his ears back and the hair on his spine standing straight up. Now he would rather sleep than investigate. A quick calculation told me that he was approaching Kelly's mother's age, if you count 7 dog years equal to one human year. I didn't want to think about that, and wiped my eyes and went to bed.

Chapter Eleven

THERE WAS A TEXT from Kelly waiting for me when I woke up the next morning. Her mother had second-degree burns from spilling boiling water on her hand when she tried to make herself a cup of tea. I didn't feel like sending endless texts or attaching cute little emojis so I called her back.

"Hi, gorgeous. Did I catch you at a bad time?" I said when she answered. I could hear her mother in the background talking. My guess is she was on her phone with one of her friends at her new home.

"No, I just finished putting new bandages on Mom, and I was going to make us a cup of tea. I assume you got my text--is that why you're calling?" I never saw the movie Ice Queen, but her tone told me she could play the lead role. Evidently, I'd read her wrong the night before. Maybe telling me that she didn't want me at the hospital was her way of saying she did. I really sucked at relationships with women. So many times, they say exactly the opposite of what they want.

"I'm sorry I didn't come up to the hospital. I thought you didn't want me there."

"It's okay, Jake. I've managed all these years without your help. I shouldn't expect it now."

"How about I make it up to you by taking you out for a nice dinner tonight? I'll tell you something that might help you get back in with Bennett."

"Save your money, Jake. There's no place nice in that hick town and I don't care what you found. As far as I'm concerned, you can tell him where to put it." I imagined her smiling at the thought.

I didn't know if she was just being mean or if she didn't care to see me right now. It was true that Truman didn't have any five-star restaurants, every one of them were mom and pops, but some did serve a decent meal from time to time. You just had to catch them on a good day.

My sad-sack moment was cut short when my phone shook me out of feeling sorry for myself. Bonnie was calling me. "Jake, I just got off the phone with Rose. She said she saw you at Fido's and that you don't think Maddie killed herself. Why don't you come over for breakfast and tell me why you changed your mind?"

· · • • •• • • • ·

"Either he's too stupid to realize the murderer wrote that text, or he wrote it himself," Bonnie said while sipping on a cup of coffee at her breakfast table later that morning. I had told her about Teller's report and the phony suicide text. I also brought her up-to-date on my meeting with Rose and Maddie's obituary. I skipped the part of my conversation with Kelly about where Bennett could shove any proof we had that Teller was wrong.

I slipped Fred a piece of my burnt sausage while Bonnie wasn't looking. "Either way, there is nothing we can do about it. We no longer have anyone we can trust at the sheriff's department."

"How long will Kelly be out?" Bonne asked, shaking her head. She had seen me feed Fred but didn't say anything.

"I don't know. She said she took a leave so she could help her mother move into assisted living. I doubt if it will be long. Sometimes, I think that job means more to her than I do."

Bonnie forced a smile as fake as the Cheshire Cat. "I think I know how to get you two back together and save her job, too."

I tried to act stunned by going completely still. "What do you have in mind, Ann Landers?"

"We find out who's behind the murders and let Kelly take the credit. Bennett will have no choice but to demote his nephew and give her the detective job."

"How do we do that, Agatha?"

"What's with all the names, Jake? Do you want my help or not?"

"Sorry, Bon. I guess Fred kept me up too long last night."

"It's no wonder, the way you're always feeding him people food. He probably had nightmares."

I didn't tell her that thinking about his age in human years was what had kept me awake all night.

I got up out of my chair to refill my coffee cup. "Anyway, I think we need to start with the first murder. Do any of your friends know who will benefit from Maddie's death?"

"It's always the husband, isn't it?" she answered, watching me pour my coffee.

"On TV, but from what I saw online, it looks like everything is in her name, so he wouldn't have anything to gain."

She handed me her cup to refill, too. "People do strange things for love. Maybe he still loved her."

"Or, more likely, hated her," I said, filling her cup halfway. I knew enough to leave room for a lot of cream and sugar. "So, we have Maddie's husband, Sheriff Bennett, Detective Teller, and that land developer who bribed Linda Jacobs at Fido's."

"Mark Adams?"

Her big cat smile was back. "You also forgot Jack Morgan."

Maybe I didn't need to worry about Fred getting old, not if his memory was anything like Bonnie's. It amazed me how she kept track of all our suspects without writing down their names.

"I suppose Morgan could still be a suspect in her death, but it's unlikely. It's obvious that whoever killed Maddie also killed Morgan."

"Not necessarily," Bonnie said as she added more sugar to her coffee. If I didn't know better, I'd think she owned stock in a sugar company. "Maybe Morgan killed Maddie and then did himself in."

I was about to answer Bonnie when we were interrupted by her phone. "It's probably another telemarketer," she said.

We listened when it went to voicemail: "Bonnie, it's Ruth. Call me back. Marge just told me that you and Jake are looking into the deaths of our commissioners. When I asked her where she heard that from, she said that Dot told her she had heard it from her daughter. Anyway, if it's true, I need to tell you about Madeline's daughter, so call me back."

"Who the heck is Dot?" I said to Bonnie before she could pick up her phone to dial her gossip friend back.

Bonnie frowned, and looked at me as if I'd just missed the one-hundred-dollar question on *Who Wants To Be A Millionaire*. "Don't be so dense, Jake. She's Kelly's mom. Marge lives in the same senior home. Now, make yourself useful and hand me my phone."

I got up to retrieve her wireless phone from its cradle on her kitchen counter and gave it to her. She punched in some numbers on the keypad and stopped. "I'll have to call her from my cell phone. I don't remember her number."

"It should be the last number on caller ID," I said, smiling. "I might not have known Kelly's mom's name, but I do know something about technology."

She called her friend back after looking at the caller ID before I could say more. "Hi, Ruth. Sorry I couldn't get to the phone in time." I couldn't hear the other end of the conversation, but I could guess that Ruth had cut her short. Bonnie tried to get a word in now and then, but Ruth wouldn't let her say anything besides, "No" or "You're kidding."

Fred got up to let himself out. He must have decided that he didn't want to watch Bonnie's hand and facial gestures any more than I did. I had installed a doggie door in the kitchen door when I had been living in Bonnie's sunroom. Would it be rude if I followed him?

Curiosity overcame boredom, so I got up to refill my coffee cup again, hoping Bonnie would get off the phone and bring me up-to-date on what Ruth had to say about Maddie's daughter. So far, what little Bonnie did say had nothing to do with the daughter. They had gone on to discuss an outfit one of their friends had worn to church.

"Well, that was interesting," she finally said to me after hanging up the phone.

"The blouse that didn't match her skirt?"

Bonnie looked at me with a blank face and rolled her eyes. "No, silly. I couldn't care less what Claire wore to church. I was talking about Maddie's daughter. She's not moving in, and the house is still for sale, so she is going to have an estate sale this weekend."

"And how is that going to help us find who's behind the killings?"

"We show up at the estate sale. We need to find a way to ask the daughter where she was the night Maddie died."

"You think her daughter might have killed her? Why would she do that?"

"Ruth says there is no mortgage on the house. It's worth a fortune, and the daughter gets everything."

"Isn't the husband the next of kin? Besides, it would still have to go through probate, and that takes time. I don't see how she can sell anything until then."

Bonnie had a mischievous gleam in her eyes like she was about to share a secret. "Maddie signed everything over to Stephanie only a month before she died."

Chapter Twelve

THERE WERE AT LEAST fifty cars parked on the road of Maddie's old house and twice that many people looking over the items spread out on makeshift tables made from saw horses with plywood tops assembled in the front yard.

I could have picked out Maddie's daughter simply based on the way she dressed, despite meeting her earlier. I'm no fashion expert, but even Fred could see that she wasn't from around here because of her clothes; they fit too well to be from the local Wal-Mart. However, the fact that she had a baby bump and was making change for a customer was the clincher. "How are you doing, Stephanie?" I asked.

She forced a smile. I had a feeling it was for show because of all the people watching us. "Jake--what are you doing here?"

I couldn't tell if she was trying to joke or be sarcastic because her smile was as phony as the fake Gucci watch she was wearing. I had become somewhat of a watch expert solving another murder case a couple of years earlier and could usually spot a cheap knockoff. The crest on her watch didn't look right.

"We're the ones who found the commissioner's body," Bonnie said to the woman who had just bought a set of dishes so she could eavesdrop. "Actually, it was Fred here who found her," I said, reaching down to pat my dog on his head. He had been sitting quietly alongside me despite all the people at the table. I cut in before Bonnie could say more. I knew her well enough to know it was her way of reacting to the rude stare the woman had given us for interrupting.

The woman's face softened. Fred had that effect on people. "What a beautiful dog, and from what the responding officer told the newspaper reporter, smart, too."

I couldn't imagine Teller saying anything nice about me or Fred, so I figured she meant Kelly. "He is that, but we don't tell him for fear it will go to his head."

Our eavesdropper chuckled, but I noticed Stephanie didn't laugh at my little joke. "I'm sorry you had to see my mother that way," she said, speaking in a flat voice as though her mind were somewhere else.

Bonnie saw her chance to put in her two cents. "I feel like I knew her personally. She was always in the news and fighting to make our community better. And if it helps, we don't think for one minute that she killed herself, and neither does Kelly."

"Kelly?" Stephanie seemed to freeze in mid-movement. " Oh...Officer Brown...Does she think someone murdered my mother?"

I had to think of a way to keep Bonnie quiet. If word got out that Kelly wasn't buying Teller's theory, she'd be in trouble with the sheriff. "I think what Mrs. Jones means is that Officer Brown had some doubts based on your mother's religion and the fact that you are expecting your first child. However, being the professional that she is, she realizes there is no way anyone could have shot her and gotten out of the room. It was completely blocked off from the inside."

Stephanie's neck and jaw tightened. "She hasn't been to church since divorcing my father and remarrying. Catholics don't allow that, you know. Besides, what you don't know is that she had terminal cancer. I think suicide was her way to escape the pain. Now if you don't mind, that woman over there wants to buy something." She held her head up high, keeping her back stiff as she walked away from us.

Bonnie was speechless, and stood with her mouth open while watching Stephanie walk away. I was about to yell out an apology when Fred decided to leave us. He must have smelled something good to eat as he had gone over to the parked cars on the road with his nose to the ground, sniffing the grass by one of the trucks.

"Fred, get over here," I yelled, going over to fetch my dog. He stopped smelling the grass and looked up at me. I could see he was deciding if he should obey or pretend that he didn't hear me calling. He chose to play deaf and went toward the front of the truck, where I couldn't see him.

I caught up with him as he was sniffing the truck's front bumper. It was one of those add-ons that looked like a cattle guard that protected the grill and headlights while allowing it to push anything out of its way.

"What's so interesting that you wouldn't come when I called you?" I asked as I reached down to attach a leash I kept in my back pocket but rarely used.

He didn't answer, so I took a closer look to see if he'd found something. I didn't see anything that would interest a golden retriever. The truck must have belonged to a redneck because of a plate with a confederate flag, a lift kit that raised it at least six inches, and tires that were wider than a tank's tread. The plate told me that the truck must be from a neighboring state because Missouri required front plates issued by the department of revenue, and this plate wasn't one of them.

I put Fred back in Bonnie's Jeep, with the windows half-open, and told him to stay. Then, I caught up with Bonnie at a table filled with crystal glassware.

She spoke first before I could tell her about the truck. "I told you she had a motive, didn't I?"

"I suppose she will make a couple thousand off the sale of all the junk out here. I hardly call that motive to kill someone."

"Junk? I'll have you know that this Depression glass is worth a small fortune, and we haven't even seen the furniture in the house yet. Don't forget that Maddie signed the house over to her just before she died."

"I'm not so sure she was murdered, Bon. Knowing she only had a few months to live, not to mention the pain she must have been in, sounds like a good reason to sign everything she owned over to her daughter before doing herself in."

"Maybe," she answered, swallowing hard and heading toward the house, "but I'm willing to bet we can find something in her bedroom that says otherwise." I looked over to see if Maddie's daughter had been watching us, then followed Bonnie when I saw that Stephanie was too busy with a customer.

Bonnie seemed to have forgotten why we had gone into the house. "That highboy would look good in my bedroom. I wonder how much Stephanie wants for it?"

"How would you ever get to the top drawers, Bon?"

"A stepstool, I guess. Do you think you can fix the scroll work? I didn't notice it the other day." She was pointing at the top of the dresser, where there was a crack in the fancy carving.

"It must have broken when Maddie tipped the highboy over to block the door," she said, frowning.

"That's a real antique, but if you're interested, I can make you a great deal," Stephanie said before I could answer. Bonnie jumped like she'd seen a ghost. We hadn't heard Stephanie come into the room. I wondered how long she'd been standing there, listening to us.

"God, you scared me. I didn't see you there," Bonnie said after catching her breath.

Stephanie continued as though Bonnie hadn't said anything. "It's been in the family for as long as I can remember. My mother said she thought her great-great-grandfather brought it with him from Boston." Her posture stiffened, and she held her nose up as though we had B.O. "Of course, I'm not going to give it away."

I decided to pull out a drawer to see if it had any maker's marks. It was something I'd seen on one of the PBS shows. There was a tag that read "Made in China."

" I didn't know China shipped to Boston back then," I said, showing her the tag.

"Let me see that." She proceeded to pull out an eyeglass case from her designer shoulder purse and open it, but not before I saw "Armani Exchange" printed on the case. "Humph. Mom had it repaired a few years back. They must have switched a drawer on her besides doing a shoddy fix on the scroll work."

"It was broken before your mother's murderer tipped it over?" Bonnie asked.

Stephanie blinked rapidly, then glared at Bonnie. "Murderer? My mom killed herself, remember? Why do you keep saying otherwise?"

Bonnie froze with her mouth half-open. She stood in shock before finding her voice, "I'm sure it can be fixed to look as good as new," she said.

Stephanie shrugged, rolled her eyes, and removed her glasses before slowly putting them back inside her purse. "Detective Teller warned me about you two. Something tells me your only interest in the highboy was to snoop. I think we're done in here." She held the door open while waving her hand for us to leave.

Stephanie locked the bedroom door, then ushered us outside. "I'll be sure to let Detective Teller know about your visit," she said, slamming her front door hard enough to shake out the broken glass in the pane I'd broken earlier, now that the plywood the sheriff had put in place was no longer there.

• • • • • • • • • •

I called Kelly from the passenger seat of Bonnie's Jeep after leaving the estate sale.

"Maybe she was just upset that you called her out on it being an antique," she said after I told her about our encounter with Stephanie.

Bonnie could hear Kelly's response because I'd connected to her Bluetooth, causing the conversation to come out over her Jeep's speakers. "If you'd been there, you'd know she's hiding something," Bonnie answered.

"Are you saying she had something to do with her mother's death?"

Bonnie smirked and curled her lips. "Does Tigger kill mice?"

"She did inherit everything, so she had a motive," I said before Bonnie could let go of the steering wheel and cross her arms.

"She needs more than motive, Jake. Her alibi checks out. She was in Belton the night Maddie died. Besides, unless someone has learned to walk through walls, Maddie took her own life. Hold on, guys, Mom needs something."

She came back to the phone in less than a minute. Just long enough for me to notice a truck come speeding up behind us. "Sorry, guys, she didn't know how to get her favorite show on TV. Now, where were we?"

"You were saying Stephanie had an alibi the night her mother died."

"I appreciate what you two are trying to do for me, I do. There is nothing more I'd like than to get something on Teller, but I think you're barking up the wrong tree."

I looked over at Bonnie and mouthed, "Did you tell her?"

Bonnie shook her head. I wasn't sure if she meant no or was saying she didn't understand.

"If you really want to help, find out who killed Jack Morgan. Teller hasn't solved that one yet. Anyway, I've got to go. Mom's back at my apartment for a few days and she's having trouble with the remote."

No sooner had I disconnected than a loud air horn blasted behind us. I turned to see the truck from the estate sale tailgating us.

Bonne opened her window and flipped off the driver. He responded with another blast of his horn.

"Pull over and let the jerk pass, Bon," I said, knowing my words would fall on deaf ears.

To my surprise, she slowed down but didn't pull over.

Another shrieking blast sounded just before I felt a tap on our rear bumper. Bonnie lost control, and her Jeep ran off the road. The truck driver gave one more long blast of his air horn before driving on.

"Are you okay?" I asked, trying not to sound upset.

She was trembling and clutching her chest. "Why did he do that?" she asked.

"Bon, switch seats with me. I think I need to get you to the hospital."

She pounded the hand she'd been holding over her chest on the steering wheel. "Did you get his license, Jake? We need to call the cops on him."

· · · ● · ● · ● · · ·

Bonnie insisted she was fine and didn't need to go to the ER. She was more concerned with Fred than she was herself. He had been asleep on the Jeep's backseat and was thrown against the rear of my seat.

We got out of her Jeep, so I could check Fred over. I couldn't feel any broken bones, and he didn't yelp when I felt his legs and back. "It looks like he's no worse for wear," I said after throwing a stick for him to fetch. He went after it and brought it back in record time.

"I wish I could say the same for my poor car," Bonnie said as she stood at the back of her Jeep, examining the rear bumper.

I walked around to where she was standing. There was a broken taillight and a dent in the bumper. "Taillights can be replaced, Bon. Let me take your Jeep to the body shop tomorrow to see how much it will cost to fix everything." My main concern was getting her to calm down before she did have a heart attack. If the color of her face was any indication, her blood pressure was higher than an overheated tea kettle.

"Don't let them do anything. Just get an estimate. I have a thousand-dollar deductible, so I'm gonna find that jerk in the truck and make him pay." She was already on her cellphone calling 911.

After the 911 dispatcher told her to file a report with the sheriff because it wasn't an emergency, Bonnie slammed her flip phone shut. "Can you believe the nerve of that woman?" she said, returning to her Jeep. "File a report? Maybe I should have said I was having a heart attack. I bet they would listen to me then."

"I'll call Kelly. Maybe she can get them to look for him," I answered, trying once more to calm her down.

• • • • • • • • •

"Do you think it was a warning of some kind, Jake? Maybe we're getting too close to the commissioners' murderer?" Bonnie regained her composure once we were back on the road, heading home.

"You watch too much TV, Bon. More likely, it was road rage."

"But it's the same truck Fred was checking out at the estate sale. He must have overheard us asking questions and followed us."

"Or he simply left shortly after we did." I didn't want to tell her that there was a possibility his road rage was for a different reason. Drug addicts don't think logically when they are high. There was a good possibility Fred might have smelled drugs in the truck, and the guy didn't like us snooping around. Because of its sparsely populated countryside and few employment opportunities, Fremont County was the meth capital of Missouri. It was easy for people to cook meth or grow pot when they lived in a house or trailer deep in the woods, where their nearest neighbor was half a mile away.

Bonnie inhaled deeply. Her nostrils were so enlarged it looked like she might exhale fire. "I still think it was a warning, but he doesn't know me very well. It will take more than a bump to scare me off."

Chapter Thirteen

FRED SAT QUIETLY BY my side when we took Bonnie's Jeep to the body shop the next day. He tilted his head as though he was listening to every word the owner of the shop was saying. Then again, he might have thought the guy I now knew as Clyde had something good to eat because of his constant chewing.

Clyde spit out his chew into a Coke bottle and wiped his mouth with his bare arm. "Your friend is looking at maybe six bills to fix the damage."

"That's a lot to take out a dent and replace a taillight," I answered. "Her thousand-dollar deductible means she'll have to pay all of it. It's going to take most of her Social Security check to pay that much." I played the poor-widow card, trying to get the price down, knowing how much these guys padded their estimates.

Clyde's weathered face softened. "You look like the kind of guy who doesn't mind getting your hands dirty, so if you want to save your friend some money, I suggest you replace that lens yourself. You should be able to find one at a junk yard cheap enough. Surely a lot less than I could get it from a dealer." The fact that I was dressed in old, torn jeans and a sweat shirt that had seen too many washes must have given him the impression that I'd be at home in a junk yard, which, of course, I would be. His remark bought back thirty-year-old memories. My first wife, Natalie, hated the time she'd waited for me outside a junk yard to pull a car part when we were first married.

Fred woke me from my flashback with a bark. "What about the bumper? That would cost a couple hundred, not to mention the work of replacing it. Can't you pop out the dent?" I asked after ruffling the fur on Fred's head.

Clyde's face tightened as his brows drew closer. "Don't hardly know," he answered, looking down without eye contact. "Ain't never done that paint-less dent removal on plastic bumpers. Now if that dent was on the sheet metal, I might let Johnny have a go at it. He does a pretty good job with the torch and dry ice."

"Dry ice?"

"Clyde smiled, then reached in his shirt pocket for his tin of tobacco. "Yeah. Works pretty good on hail dents. Johnny heats the metal with a propane torch and then throws dry ice on it.

Them dents just pop right out…most of the time, but if I was you, I'd get me a bumper from the junk yard when you get the tail light lens."

Fred lost interest when he saw what Clyde was chewing and wandered outside. I thanked Clyde for his time before joining my dog.

· · · · ●· ● · · · ·

We went back to my house after returning from the body shop. Bonnie had taken my truck and driven to the sheriff's office to file her complaint on the guy that ran her off the road, so I'd have to wait for her to return to let her know she didn't have to file an insurance claim because the Jeep could be fixed for less than her deductible. I needed to call a few junkyards about the tail light lens and bumper. I knew from experience that phone calls trumped in-person inquiries. The last time I'd been at a wrecking yard, I was made to wait while the counter person answered several phone calls.

I booted my computer to start my search for local wrecking yards. The nearest one was in Lincoln, about ten miles away, and they didn't have any Jeep tail lights or bumpers that would work. I finally found a taillight in Sedalia for only fifty dollars. They didn't have the bumper but suggested I try popping out the dent with dry ice. Did these guys have stock in frozen CO_2?

Normally, I would have driven right up there, but driving Bonnie's Jeep with a busted lens was just begging for a ticket. I decided to wait until she returned my truck. I didn't have long to wait.

Fred growled when Bonnie came down the driveway, followed by a sheriff's SUV. It could only mean the driver was someone he didn't care for.

Deputy Charlie couldn't stand still and kept fidgeting with his belt. "Detective Teller insisted I check out the damage to her Jeep before filing my report," he said while keeping a watchful eye on Fred.

He walked to the back of Bonnie's Jeep, where he took a couple of pictures with his cell phone, then opened up a notebook that had been in his shirt pocket. "Doesn't look too bad to me. Are you sure this didn't happen in a parking lot? I've seen worse damage done by a shopping cart."

"A shopping cart? Does that bumper look like a shopping cart ran into it?" Bonnie's protruding jugular vein and red face made her look as if she was going to have a stroke. "Why do you and that so-called detective refuse to see that someone is worried Jake and I are on to them?" I was afraid her dentures would pop out because of the way she bared them. I'd seen Fred do the same with his teeth when he didn't like someone, except in his case, the teeth were real and sharply pointed.

"I'm sure it's just a case of road rage, Officer," I said grabbing Bonnie by the arm. "I don't think he was trying to kill us or the damage would be a lot worse." I watched my dog in case he decided to sniff the deputy. I knew from previous encounters that Deputy Charlie didn't like dogs, which is one of the reasons I didn't trust him.

"Yeah, I see that all the time. Some people try to get a slower driver to speed up by tailgating them. He must have gotten too close."

Bonnie stared at the deputy with cold, hard eyes. "So, you're going to write this up as road rage instead of a warning to back off from our investigation?"

"Sorry, ma'am, but Detective Teller has determined there is no murder, so I don't see what the guy who supposedly ran you off the road is warning you about."

Bonnie was livid now. "What about Commissioner Morgan? Are you telling me he wasn't murdered?"

Charlie sighed, "No. Detective Teller has called that one an accident. The commissioner was cleaning his gun when it must have accidentally gone off," he said, and began writing in his notepad.

"An accident? Are you kidding?" Bonnie said, shaking her head. "Doesn't he realize Morgan was shot by the same person who killed Maddie to keep him quiet? Have you bothered to check if the same gun was used in both murders?"

Deputy Charlie took a step back and held up his palms toward Bonnie. "Whoa there, ma'am. Don't shoot the messenger. I'm only repeating what Detective Teller said based on the gun cleaning kit he found next to the body."

I needed to diffuse the conversation before it got out of hand, but luckily, Bonnie must have realized deputy Charlie hadn't made the call on Morgan's demise, and nothing she said to him would change anything. She sighed and said, "Whatever," before turning her back on the deputy and walking slowly back to her house.

Chapter Fourteen

BONNIE FINALLY CALMED DOWN after her second cup of fortified coffee. Fred and I had joined her at her kitchen table after Deputy Charlie left. I hadn't mentioned how Fred had been sniffing around the truck at the estate sale to the deputy or that I thought the reason the redneck had run us off the road might be drug-related. It was obvious that Charlie was echoing Teller's conclusion, who had his mind made up and wasn't going to listen to us.

She sat in her kitchen chair with her back bowed. "So much for helping Kelly solve this case, Freddie," she said to my dog after taking another sip of her coffee. He must have felt she needed him more than me, for he was sitting next to her with his big head on her lap.

"Actually, Bon, it works to our advantage now that Kelly is back at work." Her leave was up, and she still hadn't heard from the Highway Patrol, so she had gone back to patrolling the county roads for speeders and drunks, both of which Fremont County seemed to have more than its fair share.

Bonnie put down her cup before reaching down to pet my dog by scratching behind his ears. "How do you figure that? I mean, I know she had her heart set on leaving Bennet, and I'm glad she's not going anywhere, but I just don't see how Charlie's report is helping any."

"Well, think about it. If Teller considers both cases closed, then we don't have to worry about him solving anything before we do. We'll be able to pass what we find onto her before he knows what hit him."

Her face lit up with a smile beginning to form on her lips. "I never saw it that way, but it's perfect. You're a genius, Jake."

I looked over at Fred who was listening to our conversation. "What do you think, old boy, is your dad a genius?"

He acted as if he didn't understand me and laid his head back down without so much as a bark.

"You'd have better luck asking Tigger," Bonnie said, laughing. The cat had been lying in her bed by the sink and looked up at her mistress at the mention of her name.

I was about to ask Tigger what she thought when my cell played "Beethoven's Fifth." "Hi, Kell. What's up? Are your ears ringing?" I said, then punched the speaker phone icon so Bonnie could hear.

"Talking about me again?" She continued before I could answer. "Don't answer that. You two are already in enough trouble without lying to me."

"Oh, what did that idiot deputy tell you?" Bonnie shouted loud enough to make Tigger stand up. My phone could easily pick up voices a few feet away, and I knew she knew it. I was going to have to put less whiskey in her next cup of coffee.

"I'm reading his report now, why didn't you tell me someone ran you off the road? You could have been hurt."

"Sorry. I was going to ask you to look for him, then thought better of it. I didn't want to upset you. You have enough to worry about with your mother and everything else going on right now."

"Did Charlie mention that I thought the jerk did it as a warning?" Bonnie asked.

"No, it says it was road rage. Why do you think it was a warning, and what was he warning you about?"

I didn't want Kelly to know we were still looking for the person who we thought killed our commissioners until we had some real evidence to give her. I also didn't want Bonnie to hear about my suspicion the guy might have had drugs in the truck. "He must have been in a hurry and got annoyed at Bonnie for driving the speed limit. I think it was probably his demented way of getting her to speed up, or at least, that's my theory," I said before Bonnie could mention how she had slowed down or flipped the guy off not to mention her theory about us getting too close to the commissioner's murderer.

There was a long pause before Kelly answered, "I suppose that's possible. We do have a lot of bullies in the county. Anyway, I'll put out a BOLO on the truck. I just wanted to ask you what it looked like. Charlie neglected that in his report."

"We didn't get a good look at it on the road--the bumping happened so fast--but if it's the same truck Fred and I saw at the estate sale, you're looking for a late model pickup with a cattle guard and a Confederate flag for a front plate."

"That would describe half the trucks in the county if the plate were on the back," Kelly answered. "The truck must be registered out of state. I'll put that in the BOLO."

I gave her a few more details about the truck and driver before hanging up and turning back to Bonnie. She started petting Tigger, who had jumped into her lap the minute Fred had left to sniff the food in Tigger's bowl because Bonnie had quit scratching behind his ears. "She must believe us. That's more than I can say for that idiot, Charlie."

I tried not to grin. "I wouldn't go that far. I think he's just trying to kiss up to Teller."

She put Tigger on the floor and got up to get us fresh coffee from the pot she'd put on after coming into the kitchen.

"Whatever. So, how much do you think it will cost me to get the Jeep fixed if Kelly doesn't find the creep who ran me off the road?"

"Don't worry about that now. I can get you a taillight lens at a junk yard and put it on myself. I can't find a bumper so we're looking at buying a new one, or a knockoff on eBay. You will have to live with the dent until we find the guy who did it. What we need to think about now is who killed the commissioners so Kelly can put Teller in his place."

Bonnie stopped whatever she was doing at her kitchen counter and stared at me in awe. "She's so lucky to have you. "She opened the top drawer of her kitchen cabinet and took out a notepad and pen. "Maddie's daughter should be at the top of our list. Then put that developer you overheard who wanted the county to approve a request to build a casino on our lake," she said, throwing me the pad and pen.

"I take it you want me to start a list of potential suspects?" I said, noticing how quickly she went from complimenting me to putting me to work.

She filled our cups before putting her coffee pot back in its place. "Unless you want to be the waiter. The list of suspects is getting too long; it's time we put them on paper."

I jotted down Mark Adams and Stephanie Travers. Next, I put "developer" in quotes next to Adams' name. I smiled at Bonnie while taking the coffee she handed me before continuing, "The odds of him building a casino anytime soon are slim to none, so it makes me wonder what he really wants. Do you think it's enough to kill for?"

"From what you told me he seems like the kind of guy who wouldn't let anything, or anybody, stand in his way to get what he wanted, so yes. I think he wouldn't hesitate for a minute to eliminate anyone who was an obstacle, but if it's not a casino maybe he knows something we don't," she said after taking her chair. Tigger didn't wait a second before jumping back into her lap, and Fred went over for another ear scratch.

"Like Amazon or some other big company building here?"

She opened her mouth to speak, then paused before continuing, "I was thinking more along the lines of a tourist destination. We don't have the labor force to support an Amazon distribution center."

"Well, those are all good motives for Adams to buy up land, but I can't imagine our county commissioners giving him resistance over bringing in more jobs into the area. I think we need to look into our prime suspect," I said, making a show of getting back to our list by underlining Stephanie Travers.

"She had a lot to gain by her mother's death, but killing your own mother? I can't imagine doing that unless it was in a fit of rage."

I looked up from my list. Bonnie was pursing her lips in thought. "So, you're saying she isn't a suspect anymore?"

"No, I'm just saying I don't think it was premeditated if she did it."

"Then we can rule out the inheritance as a motive?"

"For now, at least. How about Sheriff Bennett? Surely, he had a good motive." she said, petting Tigger until she purred. It made me glad Fred wasn't a cat. I couldn't imagine having sixty-five pounds purring away on my lap.

"Bennett? You can't seriously suspect him?"

"What's so hard about putting him on the list? His affair with Maddie was quite the subject of my quilting group."

"He'd have to kill half of your gossip group to keep the affair quiet," I said.

Bonnie didn't think for a moment before answering, ignoring my remark with a shake of her head, "There is a deputy who should be on our list. Someone created the phony suicide text Maddie supposedly sent to her daughter. Is there any way you can trace those things?"

I wrote down "Sheriff Bennett," then took a sip of my coffee before answering, "Not without access to the phone company records, and that would take a warrant. Teller could have created the text simply to close the case. What motive would he have for murder?"

Bonnie tilted her head to the side like she does when she's thinking. "Maybe one of the commissioners found out about him being fired in Kansas City," she said, leaning forward in her chair. The sudden motion made Tigger yelp and jumped off her lap again.

"I'll look into it and ask Kelly if they skipped the background check on him before he was hired because he's Bennett's nephew. Even if Maddie did kill herself, the same can't be said for our other commissioner. I'm not buying that Morgan's death was an accident."

Bonnie set her coffee down on the table so she could support her chin with her right hand. I could see she was choosing her words carefully. "Wouldn't that put you back in the hot seat, Jake? You were Teller's prime suspect because someone saw you arguing with Morgan over selling your property."

"Point taken, but it's not me I worry about. Teller is out to close the case quickly so he can make a name for himself. I doubt if he cares who he throws under the bus to do it. We need to be careful that whatever evidence we find doesn't come back to hurt Kelly. I'm sure someone did Morgan in, and if Kelly can prove it, Teller will have to eat a lot of humble pie, at the very least.

"Maybe I've read and written too many murder mysteries, but I don't think any of the names on our list meet the three requirements to be a suspect. Adams may have had a motive, but where are the means and opportunity for him to knock off Morgan? The man was in Branson the night Morgan died. Bennett surely had the means and opportunity to do Maddie in, but killing her to keep her quiet? That's a pretty sketchy motive. Teller might have a motive if we can prove he has a checkered past, and that he wanted to keep it quiet. He also had means and plenty of opportunity."

Bonnie groaned. "Well, if it's motive we need, then I know the perfect suspect."

Fred felt the tension in my voice and came over to put his head on my lap. It had an immediate calming effect. "Let me guess--Maddie's husband?"

Bonnie frowned again. "I don't see him killing her. He wasn't going to inherit anything and from what I've heard, he was out of town when she was killed. No, I was thinking of the guy who ran me off the road."

I put "Redneck" on the list in quotes next to Stephanie Travers then reached down to scratch Fred behind the ears. "Maybe he's in it with Stephanie. She has the biggest motive to see her mother dead. We have to at least consider her, but I just haven't figured out why she'd kill Morgan."

Fred must have decided I was okay because he went to the living room and out his doggie door. "It's been a long day, Bon. I think we should sleep on this and pick it up tomorrow," I said, pointing to the list of suspects. I finished off my coffee before following my dog. It wasn't until later that night that I had some answers.

Chapter Fifteen

WHAT BONNIE HAD SAID about the jerk that ran us off the road had been bothering me so, I decided to give Kelly a call before going to bed. The call went straight to voicemail. "Hi, Kell. It's me. Call when you can. I was wondering if you found out any more about the guy that ran Bonnie off the road. She's going to be stuck with repairs on her Jeep if we don't find him. By the way, how are you doing? Give me a call when you can. Love ya." I ended the call, wondering if anything was wrong.

She called back before I had a chance to let my imagination run wild. "Hi, Jake. Sorry I didn't answer. I was helping Mom with her shower."

That was one subject I didn't need to know about. "I can't imagine what you're going through. How you holding up?"

"I'm fine, I guess. Between waiting to see if I get the new job and watching my mother, it's a wonder I'm still sane. I sure miss the old days when all I had to worry about was you and Fred." She let out a sigh before continuing. I imagined her sitting back in her overstuffed chair with a glass of Merlot and a faraway look in her eyes remembering the good times.

"I miss them, too. I miss you. I thought we might be spending more time together after your mother moved into assisted living. How is she, now that you've rescued her?"

"She's a lot better now that she's not taking a pill every five minutes. I swear, they must like to keep their residents sedated so they don't give them any trouble. I'm afraid moving her over there wasn't such a good idea."

Just when I'd decided this wasn't the time to ask her again about the jerk that had run Bonnie off the road, she surprised me. "By the way, Jake. I got a list of trucks that match the description of the one that hit Bonnie's Jeep."

I did a double-take and stared at the phone. It was all I could do to speak without raising my voice. "How did you do that so soon? There must be a million trucks like that in Missouri."

"Probably, but this list is for Arkansas. I reasoned that the owner was probably from there because of his front plate. I've got requests for Kansas and Oklahoma, but my gut tells me he's from Arkansas."

"Because of the Confederate plate?"

"Yes. It's highly unlikely a Jayhawk would have one of those, so I don't expect much from Kansas."

"What about Oklahoma? Do you think he could be from there?"

"Not likely, although it's on my list. Oklahoma didn't become a state until 1907, long after the Civil War. I wish you'd paid more attention to the rear plate. If I knew for sure what state it was from, I'd know where to look even without the license number."

"I wish I had checked it out, too, but I was too busy corralling Fred to walk to the back of the truck, so I could get the license number." I didn't mention the fact that it hadn't occurred to me at the time.

"Yeah, he can be a handful when he's on the hunt. Anyway, I just thought you should know. I've got to go, Mom needs me. Love you."

I told her I loved her, too, before ending the call. Fred had been watching me and looked up at me with his big, brown eyes. "She loves you, too, big boy, even if she doesn't tell us often enough."

• • • • • • • • • •

I was too wired to sleep, so I filled Fred's bowl before microwaving a TV dinner for myself, then sat down at my computer. I was way behind on my quota of five hundred words a day toward my new book. I hadn't written a word in several days but it didn't look like this was the night to catch up. I found myself browsing Facebook where I found a group called the Lakeshore Homeowners. Out of curiosity, I decided to check it out. It turned out to be homeowners in the development where I owned my property. For the next hour, I felt like Alice must have when she walked through the looking glass. I couldn't believe what I read. It was enough too put the poem "Jabberwocky" to shame.

If someone wrote a post complaining about a pothole or noisy ATVs, at least a dozen other people had to voice their opinions. In the case of the pothole, either it was too expensive to fix the roads, or they were going to hold off paying any more dues until it was fixed. For every complaint, there were several replies about why or why not something could be done. The posts I found interesting were the complaints about noisy ATVs. Madeline Summers had originated or been mentioned in most of them as she was also a home owner in the area.

Maddie had been complaining about the ATVs long before one of the neighbor kids had run over her cat. It seems they would start racing around the neighborhood on Friday nights and keep it up all weekend. She had advocated speed bumps to slow them down, but those, like the potholes, raised an endless stream of comments. People who came down from

Kansas City on the weekends and didn't live there full-time, and thought it was their God-given right to relieve the stress of the city. After all, that's why they bought homes on the lake, wasn't it?

Maddie and several other association board members disagreed. Some of the discussions became so heated I think they would have shot each other if it were possible over the Internet. I had three new suspects, and a possible fourth, I could add to my list of people who wanted Maddie out of the way. But did they want her gone badly enough to kill her? I didn't think so. However, if one of the suspects had a confrontation with Maddie, who's to say it didn't get out of hand and end violently?

Although it seemed I'd landed on a Jerry Springer podcast, there were a few posts that didn't cull negative responses. One of them was from Arnie Taggert, president of the Lakeshore Homeowners Association. Arnie had posted a collection of videos from his home security camera that included some people launching their boats at the community boat dock. He asked if anyone recognized a couple of vehicles the camera picked up.

Although it wasn't one of the trucks Arnie asked about, there was one with a cattle guard and lift kit in the parking area with a boat trailer holding a flat-bottom Jon boat with an elevated deck up front. I'd seen boats like that on the water.

They were used for shooting garfish with a bow and arrow. I couldn't see the plates because of the trailer and angle of the camera, but I'd bet my next royalty check that the front plate would be a vanity plate with a rebel flag on it. It was all I needed to pay a visit to the area. If the owner of the truck was visiting a local resident, there'd be a good chance I'd find the truck or the boat he'd been launching.

I clicked on the next video and nearly dropped the coffee I'd been sipping.

Chapter Sixteen

FRED AND I MET Kelly at Fido's the next morning to share the news about Arnie's videos. I was about to tell her what I'd found when my cell started playing "Beethoven's Fifth." "It must be from Allie. She's the only one I know young enough to text and not call," I said to Kelly. The server had just brought us our drinks and a treat for Fred.

Kelly emptied a packet of sugar substitute in her tea. I reached for my phone when Kelly started to say something but didn't. I could tell by her frown that she wasn't happy with what I'd said about texting.

I read the text aloud, hoping my remark would blow over, knowing that Kelly preferred text over voice because she was always too busy to talk. "Spring break has been canceled, and they're going to let us go home early to make up for it. Could you pick me up on the twenty-fourth? I have to move a bunch of stuff out of my dorm for the summer."

I texted back, "No problem. Should I bring the truck?" I used the phone's speech-to-text feature because of my fat fingers. Fortunately, I double-checked the text before hitting send. The text app wrote something other than truck, and it wasn't nice. I made the correction manually, added a silly heart emoji, and hit Send.

She texted back a few seconds later, "Thank U, Dad. Love U. And Goldie loves you 2." The word "Love" was a heart emoji.

"I still can't get used to the idea that you have a grown daughter, Jake. What did you do--get married at sixteen?" Evidently, my remark about texting had been forgiven.

I put a finger up to my lips, pretended to look around the cafe, and covered Fred's ears. "Twenty, but let's keep that between you and me."

Fred cocked his head to the side when I uncovered his ears, and Kelly laughed.

"How is she doing up there? Doesn't she have to take a lot of STEM classes to be a vet? I'll bet that's not easy," she said and went back to stirring her tea.

"For now. She took chemistry and biology and some electives. She really liked creative writing, so now she's thinking of changing majors. She thought I'd be happy. Little does she know that most creative writing majors never find work in their chosen field and end up flipping burgers. She could do that without a college degree."

Kelly unconsciously raised her hand to cover her mouth before speaking. "I hope you didn't tell her that. She needs to do what she wants, not what other people want her to do."

"No, not in those exact words," I said, looking down at Fred to avoid Kelly's eyes. I was saved by Kelly's phone this time.

"It's Teller, Jake. I wonder what he wants." Like my daughter, Teller had sent a text, so I had to sit still while Kelly read the message.

She closed the messaging app and put the phone back in her purse before looking at me. "He says he doesn't want me to spend any more time on Morgan's suicide. I'll tell you, Jake, the job with the Highway Patrol can't come soon enough."

The small talk was over, and time to get to the point. I looked her in the eyes. "Maybe you won't have to leave. Not if you can show that Teller isn't who he pretends to be."

She cocked her head while raising an eyebrow. "Do you know something I don't or are you just wishing?"

"It's the reason I wanted to meet with you," I said, looking around the cafe to see if anyone was listening to us before taking out my phone again. "I've got something you need to see."

She watched Arnie's video, and I watched her eyes grow bigger. "Where did you get this, Jake?"

"It's footage from the Lakeshore security cameras. Teller must not have known about them." The clip showed a truck pulling up to the lifted truck with a cattle guard in the community parking lot. The timestamp showed it was the night Fred had found Maddie dead at her farmhouse. Teller had tried to hide who he was by wearing civilian clothes and wearing a covid mask to cover his face, but even a nearsighted person couldn't miss the six-foot-five, lanky figure as he walked over to talk to the driver of the other truck.

"Is that the truck you've had me looking for?"

I simply nodded and felt a smile forming on my lips.

Kelly would have sat down if she had been standing. "So, Teller knew the guy who ran Bonnie off the road?"

"I think so, and my guess is they aren't there to play checkers."

· · · ● · ● · · · ·

After Fred and I left Fido's, we headed for Lake Shores. I didn't spot the redneck truck while driving through the neighborhood, so I went down to the community docks to see if the boat I'd seen on the video was in one of the slips. There were a couple of pontoon boats and several fishing boats but no modified Jon boats.

I came prepared with plan B so I wouldn't have to go knocking on doors. I knew from experience that it wouldn't take long for curiosity to overcome some of the neighbors, and that they would check me out if they saw a stranger in the neighborhood, so I made a show of cutting the weeds with a lawn mower I'd brought, just in case. It didn't take long.

"Looks like you're going to need something bigger than that." A middle-aged man with a beard the envy of an Amish elder was watching me from the road.

"Hi, I'm Jake," I said after going over to greet him. "You look familiar--do you live around here?"

He eyed my hand before deciding to return my gesture and shake it. "I'm Arnie. We live in the house by the water down the road. I heard you with that mower. I don't imagine that it's much help clearing this land."

"No, I guess I waited too long. Those cedars have taken hold everywhere." Red cedars grow like weeds in Missouri. Mine were too short to be called trees and too tall to cut with a lawnmower.

Fred, who had been lying under the shade of the only real tree on my property, decided to come over and check out our neighbor. I instinctively grabbed his collar, something that I found myself doing often lately. I wasn't afraid he'd bite the guy, but experience has taught me that other people don't take to dogs the way I do. I once had a neighbor who was so afraid of dogs, that he'd threatened to shoot Fred.

Arnie bent down to rub Fred's head. "Nice dog you've got there, but I'd be careful about letting him run loose. Kids in this neighborhood have been known to run over more than one pet while racing around on their ATVs. Why it was only last month that one of them hit Maddie's cat."

I feigned surprise. "Maddie?" I asked, taking a step back.

Arnie's face softened. "Our late county commissioner? She was my next-door neighbor before killing herself in her mother's old house," he said while stroking his beard with his left hand. I was glad he had shaken my hand with his right hand when I saw crumbs from his breakfast drop to the ground.

I blinked several times. "Madeline Summers was your neighbor?"

"Yeah. We shared a dock. Well, it's her dock, but she let me put my fishing boat in it. She rarely used her pontoon and had no need for the second slip. About the only time she took the pontoon out was when her sister's grandkids came down from the city. I suppose I'll have to move my boat when the new owners take over."

He took a couple of deep breaths and forced a smile. I could see he wasn't finished. "Which brings me back to your property. I was hoping you might want to sell it. I barely have room to park my car on my property, the lakefront lots are only fifty feet wide, and your lots are close enough that I could store my boat over here. I might even build one of those pole barns to keep it out of the weather."

He had drawn himself up to his full height before making his offer. If he was trying to intimidate me, it didn't work. Even at his full height, which must have been around five-ten, I could see the top of his balding head. "Wow. That's the second offer I've had this month."

His posture stiffened, but it failed to make him any taller. "Oh? Someone else made you an offer? Mind me asking who?" he asked, kneading his beard again.

The thought ran through my head that if he didn't leave the scraggly growth on his face alone, it was going to fall off. "Another of our county's finest, Jack Morgan."

"Well, I don't have to worry about that offer, do I? I wonder why he wanted those worthless lots?" Then before I could reply, he seemed to realize he might have offended me. "I'm sorry. I didn't mean it the way it came out. It's just that I knew the previous owner, and he didn't think much of the area. I guess that's why he let the county take them for back taxes. I could shoot myself for not buying them when they came up for auction."

"Don't worry," I said, thinking that maybe my lots weren't worth as much as I'd thought they were. He was the second person this month to say they were worthless. "They didn't sell at auction, and I picked them up at the third filing. So, I guess nobody thought they were worth much if it took three years before they sold."

He sighed again and put out a hand toward Fred. "Well, if you ever do decide to sell, please let me know. I'm sure I can offer more than Jack did. Not to speak ill of the dead, but he did like to low-ball people."

I could see that Arnie was about to leave. I couldn't let him do that until I found out about the truck. "Well, I could use the money to buy a newer truck. Mine is worn out. You wouldn't know someone willing to sell one, would you?"

He removed the KC baseball cap he was wearing and wiped his forehead. "Old Jim might be willing to sell his Ford. He took it back from his nephew a couple days ago. Had to drive all the way to Yellville to get it back, and he don't have no use for two trucks."

"Oh?" I said, trying my hardest not to thrust a fist into the air. "That's in Arkansas, isn't it?"

Arnie rocked back on his heels and rolled his eyes as if I'd asked a dumb question. "Yeah. I helped him bring it back. Had to drive nearly two hundred miles each way.

"He lives over on Redbud if you want to stop by and talk to him about it. I'll call him and let him know you're coming and tell him to give you a good price. Call me if you guys make a deal, and I'll take these lots off your hands." Arnie patted Fred on the head and left.

We both watched Arnie walk down our road toward his house. Fred looked up at me as if to ask, *What was that all about*? I swear, sometimes he understands English just fine.

Arnie was almost home when out of nowhere an ATV came roaring down the road. He had to jump in order not to be hit. The kid driving the machine was looking back over his shoulder at another four-wheeler hot on his heels. Arnie yelled something at the kids as they raced by, but I doubt if they heard him over the noise of their unmuffled machines.

Chapter Seventeen

I MUST HAVE MISSED Old Jim's house and the street he lived on during my first search for his house, so I asked Siri for directions to Redbud Street in Lake Shores, Missouri. She displayed a map of a development fifty miles from here and asked me if that was what I wanted. I shook my head and closed the app. Sometimes I really missed the old-fashioned paper maps but I knew that few people even knew how to read one of those anymore. It looked like I'd have to do it the way my ancestors did and drive around looking for the street. At least I knew the street I had to look for now.

Fred had his head out the window as we drove up and down the neighborhood looking for Redbud Street or Drive or whatever it was called. After driving up and down the same streets several times, I thought about asking Siri again but thought better of it when one of the residents came out of his house, shaking his head.

The guy looked to be somewhere south of sixty with a military-style haircut. "You looking for anyone in particular?" he asked as I pulled over to talk.

"Someone by the name of Jim who lives on Redbud Street," I answered after leaning out Fred's open window only to get a wet dog tongue on my face.

He approached my truck and offered a hand, palm up, for Fred to sniff before patting him on the head. "We got two Jims who live on Rosebud. Any idea which one you want?"

"He drives a newer Ford pickup if that helps."

"Yeah. I heard he had to take that back from his nephew after the kid fell behind on the payments. I told Jim it was a bad idea to cosign for him. That worthless kid hasn't worked in months."

The guy seemed like he couldn't wait to tell me the gossip about Jim and his nephew, so I turned off the ignition. "What kind of work did the nephew do when he had a job? I've been looking for someone to help on the farm I manage--maybe he'll be interested."

My new friend laughed, showing his nicotine-stained teeth. By the grin on his face, it looked like I'd just auditioned for a standup comedy show. "Unless you're growing pot on that farm, I doubt if he'd give you the time of day. That worthless kid hasn't done nothin' since his meal ticket killed herself."

"Madeline Summers?"

He leaned against my door, only inches from my face. Thank God Fred decided to stick his big head out the window so Yellow-teeth couldn't see my nose twitch. I didn't want to offend him, at least not until I heard what he had to say about Maddie. "Did you know her?"

"Kind of. If you call being one of them gigolos work."

I could feel my mouth fall open, "They were an item?"

"More or less. A lot less in his case, or so I hear," he said between telling Fred what a good boy he was and rubbing his head.

"Anyways, you want to turn right at the next road and follow that down to the second road. Turn left there and go about half a mile, and you'll see a dirt road on the left. It looks like an overgrown driveway 'cause the two Jims don't go that way much."

He must have seen the frown growing on my face and added, "Though, it's a lot easier to get to from Cedar Street. Redbud comes off Cedar. You can't miss old Jim's house. He's the one with all the junk in his yard," he said before giving Fred another pat on the head and turning back toward his house. I had visions of Pig Pen from the Charlie Brown cartoon walking in a cloud of dirt and dust following him.

· · ● ● · ● ● ● · ·

We found Old Jim's house a half-hour later. I got lost again trying to follow directions from Fred's new friend and accidentally saw Cedar Street cross one of the roads I was on. I went down Cedar two blocks to Rosebud and wondered if I should have left breadcrumbs to find my way back. I knew it was the right Jim, not because of the junk in his yard, almost everyone had their share of that, but because of the pickup sitting on the lawn with a Confederate flag on its front plate.

Fred went over to sniff Jim's truck when I went to the front door of the house. When nobody answered my knock or when I called out loud, I went over to the truck, too.

"What do you think, big boy--is this the same truck you saw at the auction?"

He looked up at me and barked. I took that as a yes and reached for my cell phone.

"Hi, gorgeous," I said as I went to the rear of the truck when Kelly's voicemail finished playing her recorded message. "We found the truck that ran Bonnie off the road, and you were right about the rear plate. The truck is from Arkansas." I took a picture of the plate number and sent it to her before rejoining Fred who was sniffing the ground at the passenger door. I was about to ask him what he'd found when I heard the sound of a shell being chambered into a shotgun.

Chapter Eighteen

"YOU BETTER HAVE A good reason to be trespassing on my property, mister." Someone said behind me.

I turned slowly to see a gray-haired man with bib overalls and a shotgun pointed at my head. "Whoa there, buddy," I said, holding up one hand while reaching for Fred's collar with my other. "Arnie told me you might be interested in selling this truck. We were just checking it out is all. He was supposed to call you."

"Ain't never got no call from Arnie or nobody. I forgot to charge my phone last night," he answered, lowering his gun. "So, you lookin' to buy a truck?"

The hair on Fred's back stood up when Jim had chambered his shotgun, making me glad I'd decided to grab his collar before he'd gone on the offensive. "Yeah, this one looks a lot nicer than the piece of junk I own. Is it for sale?"

Jim came over toward us with a grin on his face. "If the price is right," he said as if he hadn't just threatened to shoot us.

"Too bad you put that lift kit on it. The lady I work for would have a hard time climbing into it. I'd have to do something about that."

"That was my nephew's idear. Kids nowadays think it's cool, I guess." He answered while scratching the three-day growth on his chin as though he was deciding if I was really interested or just making excuses for trespassing.

"I see it also has Arkansas plates. I suppose the title is out of state as well?"

"Ain't no problem. All you need is a VIN check by the Highway Patrol or an inspection station. I know someone who can do that for you, but the bank has to release the lien before you can get a title. We can do all that in their office if you have the cash."

"That depends on how much you want for it." He didn't need to know I had all of twenty-three dollars to my name until Amazon made their monthly royalty deposit into my bank account, which wouldn't come close to paying for the truck.

"Fifteen thousand, and I'll have the kid put the original springs back on." He scratched his stubble again while chewing on his lower lip. "Of course, I'd have to see something upfront before I do that."

"Is your nephew here? I thought he lived in Arkansas."

He stopped scratching his chin and narrowed his eyes, almost squinting. "Why you so interested in Carl? Do you want the truck or not?"

At least now I had a first name for the truck driver who'd run Bonnie off the road. "Yeah, I'm interested. It's a little more than I have in the bank, so I'd have to raise the rest first. How about you give me your number, and I'll call you when I get it?"

Old Jim shook his head before turning his back on us and walking to his house. "Come on by when you got the money. I got better things to do than waste my time on you," he said as he left.

· · · · ● · ● · · ·

I waited until I was on the main road out of Lake Shores before calling Kelly. Her phone went to voicemail again, so I left her a message about the truck and that the guy we were looking for was named Carl. I'm sure, with her connections, she could run a check on the license number and get his last name.

Kelly called me after I'd returned home and let Fred out to do his thing. "I got your messages, Jake. Sorry I didn't answer. You should have called the front office." She sounded tired.

"I was afraid Teller would get wind of me sticking my nose into his case," I answered.

"What case? He closed it, remember? Sorry about that. It's just that you caught me at a bad time. How about I come over after my shift is over and I make sure Mom is okay? We can talk about it then."

I had a vision of us snuggling on the couch with a bowl of popcorn and watching an old movie later when I went outside to join my dog after Kelly's call. I needed someone who didn't question everything I did after realizing she probably wanted to tell me to butt out of the investigation. Unfortunately, Bonnie pulled into her drive before I could run it by Fred.

"You look like something the cat dragged in. What's wrong, Jake?" she asked after going to the back of her Jeep and grabbing a bag of groceries. I walked over with Fred to help her.

I took the bag she had in her arms and one more from the back of the Jeep. "Fred and I found the truck that ran you off the road and I called Kelly to tell her about it. She acted like she could care less."

Bonnie frowned and forced a laugh. "Couldn't care less." The years she'd spent teaching high school English were ingrained into her too deeply to ignore my slip of the tongue.

"I find the guy who almost killed us, and all you can do is correct my grammar?"

She lowered her head and reached out for Fred. "Sorry, Jake," she said, holding Fred's head between her hands. It looked as if she were apologizing to him instead of me. "I do that when I get nervous."

I was on the third step leading to the porch and stopped to look at her. "Are you feeling okay?"

She smiled and waved me on. "I need to get ready for my bridge club. Rose is so critical of everything I do, it makes me nervous. Now, take those groceries to the kitchen so I can get ready. Then you can tell me what's got you so upset."

"I'm worried about Kelly, is all. I shouldn't take it out on you," I replied and headed for her front door with the grocery bags in my arms.

· · · ● · ● · · ·

Bonnie had forgiven me for being short with her after her second or third cup of coffee. She had gone straight to making coffee after joining Fred and me and was now sitting at her kitchen table, fixing her coffee with Tigger on her lap.

"So, anyway," I said after watching her stir in the third spoonful of sugar, "after seeing the video on Facebook, Fred and I went over to Lake Shores to see if we could find the truck.

The president of the association came over to talk to us. That's when I learned who owned the truck, so Fred and I went to see him. I'll tell you, Bon, Old Jim is a piece of work. He acts like a hick, but that guy is sharp. He saw right through my charade of wanting to buy the truck."

"And you think his nephew, Carl, is living with him?"

"Or close by. Did I tell you he and Maddie were having some kind of affair?"

Bonnie slammed her cup on the table and covered her mouth with the palm of her hand. "No way! He must be half her age, or was."

"According to the Lake Shores president, Carl was some kind of gigolo."

"Wow, first the sheriff and now the redneck. I wonder who else she was sleeping with? But that doesn't explain why he was at the estate sale." She blinked and tilted her head to one side. "What did he have to gain by being there when all the proceeds will go to her daughter, and why did he follow us and run me off the road?"

I lowered my gaze and pretended to study my coffee. "There is something I forgot to tell you about the day we were at the auction."

"Oh?" she said, much the same way she must have to a student after claiming his dog had eaten his homework.

"Fred was sniffing around his truck. I think he smelled drugs."

Bonnie shook her head, but she didn't miss a beat. She didn't seem at all upset that Carl might be a drug dealer. It made me wonder why I hadn't told her about the drugs sooner. "That might explain why he ran me off the road. He was probably trying to show us that he could be dangerous, but it doesn't explain why he was at the auction."

"Don't murderers always return to the scene of the crime?"

"You've been reading too many murder mysteries, Jake. I wouldn't want to go anywhere near where I killed someone," she answered, getting up slowly from her chair.

I suppressed a laugh when I tried to picture Bonnie killing someone. "Maybe there was something he wanted to bid on that meant something to him?" I had expected her to be upset with me for not telling her about the drugs and found myself thinking out loud, looking for an answer to her question.

Bonnie went to the kitchen counter and took the pot out of the coffee maker. "Like something he might have given her and wanted it back? She refilled my cup and then filled hers halfway, leaving room for cream and sugar. I wanted to tell her to go easy on the sugar but knew better than to give advice to a woman my mother's age.

I was saved from making that mistake by Fred's bark. He heard something outside and rushed out the doggy door before I could say anything I'd be sorry for. He came back a few minutes later, wagging his tail and followed by most of Bonnie's Friday night bridge club. Rose must have been running late.

Fred and I said our goodbyes and went home before she showed up. I wasn't in the mood to talk to anyone, even my number one fan.

I texted Kelly on our way back to my place. Although my culinary skills consisted of microwave dinners, I did know how to barbeque, and I promised her I'd cook her favorite chicken breasts if she'd bring the side dishes. Maybe we'd have that popcorn and movie after all.

Chapter Nineteen

WE WERE CLEANING UP the last of the dishes when I brought up the subject of finding Carl by tracking Old Jim with a homemade GPS tracking device. "I think he's hiding something, Kell," I said, placing dishes in the dishwasher after she had already cleaned them in the sink. It was a habit both she and Bonnie had that drove me crazy. Luckily, I was on a well, and it wasn't really a waste of water.

She handed me a wine glass to put into the dishwasher that was cleaner than when I'd poured her favorite Merlot in it an hour earlier. "He's just protecting his nephew, Jake."

"I don't think the kid means that much to him. Not the way he talked, anyway, but I think we can use the phone to find Carl."

"I'm not sure finding him will do much good. The best I can charge him with is a misdemeanor for leaving the scene of an accident. And if Carl is in Arkansas, I won't even be able to do that."

"What about switching plates? Isn't that a felony?"

"No, that's a misdemeanor, too," she said while leaving me at the sink to join Fred on my couch. My living room was just an extension of the kitchen with a recliner, couch, and coffee table facing a flat-screen TV on the opposite wall. It was well within hearing distance of the sink.

I put the last dish into the dishwasher and went to join her and my dog. Fred must not have liked Kelly and me sitting too close on the couch, he wiggled his way between us and put his head in her lap so she would pay more attention to him than me.

She laughed at his antics and looked up at me, wrinkling her nose. "Tell me about this homemade GPS thingy you've come up with. It sounds a lot more complicated than just buying one off the shelf," she said while scratching Fred behind the ears. It made me wonder if she had any idea the effect of her making that face had on me.

"Those require a monthly service fee to the GPS provider. I did my research and found out that I could use an old Android phone I have by simply installing some software on it and my phone. That won't cost much, if anything, either. Then, all I need to do is attach it to Carl's truck and wait for him to come and get it. The software will alert me when the truck is moving and show me exactly where it goes and how it got there."

"Okay, MacGyver, forget I asked. It sounds like you may be in a gray area I don't need to know about. I believe you need a person's consent to install a GPS tracking device on their vehicle, so I didn't hear a thing you said." She had stopped scratching Fred and was now gazing into my eyes.

Fred got the message that she was finished, got off the couch, and went over to his bowl to get a drink.

Kelly reached over and let her fingers trace a scar on my face. "I've got another hour before Mom's caregiver expects me back," she said and leaned in for a kiss.

I started to return the kiss when Fred interrupted by rushing to the front door, wagging his tale like a horse swatting flies. "Hope we're not interrupting anything," Bonnie said. She and my daughter barged in without knocking.

Kelly jumped off the couch, closing the top buttons of her blouse. "Allie! It's so good to see you," she said, rushing over to hug my daughter.

Allie hugged Kelly back, then turned her head toward me. "I thought I'd surprise Dad. I wanted to see him before going to Colorado for the summer."

Bonnie smiled and leaned toward my daughter. "You surprised me, too, kiddo. If I'd known you were coming, I'd have had my bridge group stay longer so I could show them how much you've grown."

"I thought I was supposed to pick you up next week?" I said when I got my turn to hug my daughter.

"Jen let me store my things in her parents' garage for the summer, so I thought I'd save you the trip and surprise you," she said after I released her from my grip.

"Well, I'm happy you did, but not as glad as Fred." He had gone over to greet Goldie, Allie's dog, who was sitting quietly at her side.

"By the looks of things, we should have called first, or at least knocked." Bonnie was looking at Kelly. Her smile was now a huge grin.

I ignored her comment and changed the subject. "I see you've been training Goldie. I wish I could get Fred to behave like that."

Allie didn't answer. Kelly was already dragging her away toward my tiny kitchen table. "You've got to tell me all about school and any boyfriends you have."

Bonnie wasn't about to miss any gossip and joined them, along with Fred and Goldie. I did what any guy in a room full of women would do and started a fresh pot of coffee.

"Jake tells me you want to be a vet, and you're taking pre-med classes," Kelly said while sitting across from my daughter, listening to every word she said.

Allie gazed in my direction for a moment, then lowered her eyes without looking at Kelly. "Oh, I guess I didn't tell Dad yet. I switched majors. I think I want to go to law school after I finish my undergrad work."

I started to say something but was interrupted by Bonnie, who was nodding vigorously. "I think that's wonderful. You should follow your heart and do what you want, not what others think you should do."

"I couldn't agree more," Kelly added. I was outvoted. I'm sure if Goldie could talk, she would have supported my daughter's decision, too.

"My poly sci professor thinks so, too," Allied said. "He's even offered me a part-time internship."

I made a mental note to check out this professor, but in the meantime, I kept my mouth shut.

· · · ●·●·● · ·

The women left three hours later after my daughter had brought everyone up-to-date on everything from her latest hair color to the guys her friends were dating. Fred and I had tried to keep up, but I finally fell asleep on the couch with Fred at my feet. We awoke when Kelly kissed me on the forehead and said goodnight.

Moments later, the women were on their way out the door, with Bonnie insisting Allie stay in her spare bedroom.

Chapter Twenty

I'D DECIDED NOT TO use a phone that could be traced back to me for my homemade GPS tracker, and bought a cheap burner phone with cash a few days later. It took me less than an hour to install the chip and software. I was ready to put my plan of tracking Carl in motion. Now all I needed to do was attach it to Carl's truck.

I had brought Allie up to date on my new investigation and my latest suspect. "I've really missed all of this," Allie said as I put the phone in a bag along with some rebar wire, a wire cutter, and duct tape. Bonnie had to go to her quilting club, and Allie didn't feel like joining her, so she had come over to spend some time with Fred and me instead.

"We missed you, too, honey," I said, glancing at my dog who was more interested in his old friend, Goldie, than us. They were both in the kitchen, sharing his food. "But it's important that you get a good education. Sleuthing doesn't pay all that well." I didn't mention that waiting the counter at McDonald's didn't pay well either. I didn't believe a political science degree would get her much of a job once she graduated, but I could be wrong now.

She slowly shook her head in frustration. "I can't believe the sheriff promoted this other guy over Kelly. She's so smart," she said, swallowing hard as she watched me stuff my bag.

"It's why Bonnie and I decided to find out who's behind these murders. If Kelly can show Bennett they weren't a suicide and accident, he'll have to fire Teller and give her the detective job."

Allie bit her lip while twisting her hair around her index finger. "If she's still working as a deputy. Bonnie told me she's applied for a job with the Highway Patrol."

"All the more reason we need to solve this case for her and soon," I answered, wondering if I should say something about her hair. She had died part of it pink."

Allie shifted in her chair and straightened her posture. "Count me and Goldie in, Dad. We're not going anywhere until we find him."

"I thought you said you were going to Colorado for the summer."

"Mom will have to wait."

"She won't be a happy camper. I've never known your mother to wait for anyone."

Allie frowned and hung her head.

Goldie must have sensed the change in temperature and left Fred so she could check on her mistress. She sat next to her and tried to stick her wet snout in Allie's left hand.

It seemed to have the desired effect. Allie raised her head, showing a slight smile. "Well, I'm an adult now, so she can't tell me what to do."

I held off saying how Natalie would have something to say about our daughter's new hair-do and simply nodded, wondering if I should warn my ex.

· · · · ●· ● ● · · ·

Luckily, Old Jim didn't have any dogs or he might have been alerted when I snuck back later that night to plant my home-made GPS tracking device.

Bonnie and Allie dropped me off on Cedar Street so I could approach Old Jim's on foot. I'd brought Fred, as his sense of smell and hearing was much better than mine. I figured he'd alert me if Jim should hear me messing with his truck.

The moon was half full, giving me just enough light to find our way along the dirt road leading to Jim's house. I was surprised to see the truck was gone and no longer sitting on the lawn where it had been the last time we were here. It could mean that either Old Jim wasn't home or his nephew had come for it. Either way, it didn't look good. I was about to leave when I heard the beat of rap music coming down the road.

I was beginning to doubt my wisdom of bringing Fred as we ducked behind a storage shed and waited. If he should decide to bark, I'd be as good as dead. Visions of Old Jim's loaded shotgun ran through my head. Seconds later, I saw the outline of a cattleguard through neon headlights. I ducked behind the shed just in time to avoid the lights revealing our position, and looked down at my partner in crime. I prayed no cat or squirrel would show up, and whispered for him to be quiet.

The driver of the truck parked in the gravel drive next to the house, and the music stopped. I peeked around the corner of the shed when I heard footsteps on the stairs going into the house and then the slamming of a door. Fred squirmed out from my grip on his neck but didn't bark or run after the truck's driver.

Lights went on inside the house, so I hurried over toward the truck and slid underneath. Fred followed and slithered in next to me. I put my finger to my lips, hoping he understood to keep quiet, and then felt around for someplace to attach my tracker. It needed to be someplace away from rocks or gravel that might be thrown up by the truck's tires, and it couldn't be too close to the muffler or wheels, which didn't leave many options. I should have thought this out ahead of time. Then I checked to see if the spare was under the truck and got lucky when I found a full-size tire and wheel toward the back. It was suspended horizontally from the bed of the truck on a cable. I was able to place my cell phone tracker on top of the spare by taping it in place with some of the duct tape I'd brought along. I was almost finished when Fred started growling.

"I tell you, boy, I don't want no part of this anymore. That guy who was here has a girlfriend who's a cop. If she gets wind of any of this, it's over." Bringing Fred wasn't such a great idea. I reached over and grabbed his collar and was ready to grab his mouth if he let out another sound.

"And I told you, Uncle, I'll take care of it. Soon, neither one of them will be sticking their noses into this deal."

"That's what you said last week, and all you accomplished by running him and that old biddy off the road was to bring him snooping around here."

I couldn't see the two from under the truck and there was no way I was going to get back to the safety of the storage shed without being seen. I needed a distraction to get them away from the truck, so I pulled out my cell phone and texted Bonnie. Texting her was the best idea I could think of, assuming she would read it.

It seemed like forever, but a few seconds later, I heard the sound of her horn. "What the..." Carl said when he heard it.

The next sound I heard was the click of a shotgun shell being chambered in Old Jim's gun. They were both off the porch and headed toward the sound of the horn before I had the chance to thank the Lord. I finished attaching my GPS tracker and slid out from under the truck, still holding Fred's collar. Once we were past the shed, I let him go and kept running down the dirt road away from Cedar Street. Luckily, he followed me instead of going after Carl and his uncle.

When we were out of sight of the house and truck, I stopped long enough to call Bonnie, who picked up on the second ring. "Bon! Get out of there. They're coming to see what all the noise is about!"

"Already left, Jake. Can you make it to the other road? I'll pick you up over there."

"We're on our way," I said and disconnected. My hope now was that she would remember how to find Mulberry Street. I'd shown her the escape route on Google Maps beforehand in case we needed it.

· · · • · • • · · ·

"That was exciting, Dad," Allie said when we were back at Bonnie's. Her eyes were sparkling and it looked like she was about to squeal.

Bonnie turned around from her kitchen counter and pretended to fan herself. "Oh? I found it terrifying, especially when I couldn't remember how to get back to Mulberry. Thank God Allie remembered."

I looked over at my daughter and smiled, only to see her freeze in mid-sentence "He's coming here," she said, looking at the map of my GPS tracker on her cell phone.

Chapter Twenty-one

WE ALL WATCHED GOOGLE Maps in real-time where we saw Carl's truck as it came down our road.

"Oh, my God--he's coming here," Bonnie said and ran into her bedroom.

Both goldens must have felt the tension in the room as they headed for the front door. I managed to head them off and lock their doggie door before they could escape. The last thing we needed was for either of them to be shot by Old Jim or Carl.

Allie must have been thinking the same thing as she reached for her cell phone. I could only assume she was about to call 911.

"You can put that away, Allie," I said, pointing to my phone. "He's not coming here. The GPS tracking map showed him continuing down our road.

Bonnie came out of her bedroom with a shotgun in her hand at the same time that Allie put down her phone.

"It's okay, Bon. He's going to Maddie's," I said when Google Maps showed the truck turn into the driveway of Madeline's family homestead.

"What do you think he's doing at Maddie's?" she asked, ignoring me while loading two more shells in the gun.

Allie's eyes were as big as silver dollars. Her mother had never allowed me to have a gun in the house, so I assumed this was the first time she'd seen one up close. Seeing Bonnie handle the firearm as if it were just another kitchen implement must have been a shock to her. "Do you know how to use that?" she asked Bonnie.

Bonnie chuckled, displaying a wide grin. "Does Tigger like mice? My father made sure the girls in my family knew how to handle guns so it was second nature. Like Goldie there, knowing how to swim," she said, nodding at Goldie. "And if Carl thinks otherwise, he's in for a surprise. I've loaded it with double ought buckshot."

"Getting back to your question, Bon, I have no idea what he's doing at the house. My guess is he's looking for something. It's probably the reason we saw him at the estate sale."

"Should we call Kelly and tell her?" Allie asked, her eyes still as big as one of the girls in a Keane painting.

Bonnie curled her lip and smirked while stroking the stock of her shotgun. "I say we go over there and catch him in the act. We can call Kelly later."

I reached over and pushed the barrel of her gun down. "We have no authority to make an arrest, and I'm sure he'll be gone before Kelly can get there. Let's hold off on doing anything foolish and wait to see where he goes next. We can call Kelly then." I needed to calm her down before she worked herself up to where her blood pressure caused a vessel to burst.

She put the gun down and headed for the kitchen. "You're no fun, Jake. I'm going to put on a pot of coffee."

. . . .

Allie kept her eyes on the Google map while we all sat around the table, drinking our coffee. It looked as if Carl wasn't about to leave any time soon, and I almost dozed off like Fred and Goldie when the truck started to move again. It went past Bonnie's, toward Lakeshore, and parked in North Shores on Rosebud Street, back at Old Jim's.

We took turns watching the phone's screen, and after we hadn't seen any movement of the truck for over an hour, I finally decided to call it a night. "It looks like he's in for the night, and I think we should all go to bed, too."

Allie sipped her coffee. Like Bonnie, she had added cream and sugar to mask the taste of black coffee. I knew she would rather have a cappuccino or latte as she wasn't a real coffee drinker. "I wonder if he found what he was looking for?" she said, tilting her head to the side.

Bonnie held her cup with both hands and spoke in a steady voice. "I still think we should go over there to see what he was doing."

"And how do we do that?" I asked, surprised the women weren't ready to turn in. "It's not like we could tell if he took anything. We don't know what was left in there after the estate sale, or even if he moved anything because we have no idea where things were before he went over there."

"Isn't the place up for sale now?" Allie said.

Bonnie took a sip from her cup, then cleared her throat. "Are you suggesting we buy the place so we can look inside?"

Allie lowered her head as though she had just given a wrong answer in a high school math class.

"Or pretend to," I said when I saw my daughter's woeful look. I sat back in my chair and held my hands behind my head. "Maybe it's time to call a real realtor?"

Allie's funk was quickly replaced with a wrinkling of the nose and raised eyebrows. "You have unlicensed realtors here?"

"That's a story for another time," Bonnie answered.

I smiled, remembering when we had pretended to be realtors/inspectors.

I called Stephanie's listing agent the next morning, pretending that Bonnie's sister was interested in Maddie's house.

· · · ● ● · ● ● ● · ·

Gloria stared at me with her dark brown eyes as though she could see the lie I told to get her to show us the house. "I hear you were the one who found the body," she said after fetching a key from the lockbox and unlocking the front door. I pretended to check my messages while taking a video of her punching in the lockbox code, noticing that someone had replaced the glass in the door I'd broken to gain access when I rescued Tigger.

"Wasn't it Fred who found the body, Dad?" Allie said, instinctively reaching down to pet his head. Bonnie wanted to come too, but she had a church council meeting that I didn't find out about until after I'd made an appointment to see the house with the real estate agent listing whose name I had seen on the sign outside the house.

"Well, actually Fred helped us find Ms. Summers. Bonnie and I were out searching for her cat when Fred either smelled or heard her and led us to the house," I said, making a mental note of the lockbox. I had expected it to be tampered with, so

Carl either knew the combination or he'd gained entry to the house some other way. Of course, there was the possibility that he hadn't entered at all.

"Bonnie?" Her voice trailed off, and her eyes went up as if she was trying to put a face to the name.

"Bonnie Jones. I think she goes to the same church as your aunt and uncle. She's the one who recommended I call you." It was the best I could think of, as Gloria's name was hard to miss on the For Sale sign in front of the house. She was also the agent that had been assigned by the probate court. As was the case with most things in a small town, she just happened to be the probate judge's niece.

"Oh, her. Well, why don't we go on in and take a look?" she said after narrowing her eyes and pushing the front door open. If the hinges had been looser, the door's handle would have made a hole in the wall when it slammed into it.

I stood in the foyer pretending to check out the detail of the wainscoting, trying to remember where the furniture had been now that the living room was empty. The bare room looked much larger than when Bonnie and I had been there before. I wanted to go straight to the bedroom where Fred had found the body, but I went toward the kitchen instead. I needed the charade of being interested in the house to seem real. Kitchens are what sell a house, or so I read somewhere, and the bedroom would have to wait. If there was any sign of blood in there, it would definitely affect the selling price of the home.

"I take it the kitchen is closed off from the rest of the house with a door to hide it from any visitors?" I said, heading off to the back of the house and acting as if I was truly interested in buying the place.

"That is one of the charms of these old Victorians. People of means had servants who were kept out of sight. All of the cooking went on behind closed doors."

I opened the kitchen door, and we stepped inside.

I was shocked. I'd been too occupied with the stairs leading to the basement the last time I'd been in the kitchen and hadn't noticed the upgrades. I half expected to see a wood-burning stove and icebox, but the appliances were modern. There was a refrigerator built into the wall cabinets, along with a double oven, straight out of one of those home remodeling shows on TV. It also had a huge farm-style sink in the counter along the adjacent wall. A gas stove with its own water faucet finished off the updated appliances. Someone had spent a fortune remodeling this kitchen. It made me wonder why it had been abandoned.

"Wow," I said after the shock of seeing a kitchen bigger than my entire living room. "It looks like she didn't spare a penny on this remodel. I wonder why the rest of the house is so run down."

Gloria's body stiffened and she took a step back. "I thought you hadn't seen anything but the bedroom when you found Maddie's body?"

"We didn't. The cops showed up before we could call them and made us leave. I assumed the rest of the house was a reflection of the outside. You have to admit, it will take a lot of work, not to mention money, for new siding and a roof. Then there's the foundation, septic, and water well. If any of those are bad, it could cost a king's ransom to fix or replace." I found myself rattling. It was a habit I had when nervous.

Gloria's shoulders seemed to relax. "I think she was in the process of fixing the old place up so she could move in. I heard she was having some kind of feud with the neighbors where she was living and wanted to move." A grin formed on her lips. "Women always start a remodel in the kitchen, you know." She finished by brushing her hair back and gave me what looked like a wink. Was she flirting with me or showing off her two-carat diamond ring?

"That's where Mom started remodeling after you left, Dad," Allie said softly, with a distant look in her eyes. She had been ten at the time Natalie and I divorced. It was a bad age for any kid to lose their father.

I tried to change the subject, hoping to cheer her up. "Yeah. Most of my remodels start there, at least the ones run by the wives," I answered.

Gloria rolled her eyes, trying to look superior. "Of course, they do. It slipped my mind that you dabble as a handyman on the side. I almost forgot after reading your author page on Facebook. I hope your handyman skills are better than your marketing skills. That page does nothing for me, but we are always looking for someone to work on our listings if you ever decide to give up writing."

I shook my head slowly, trying not to respond to the obvious insult, remembering why I was here. "I'm afraid I will have my hands full if I buy this place, but before I can even consider making an offer, I'll need someone to check out the well and septic. Those are something we'll need a professional opinion on unless there is some kind of recourse if they turn out bad."

"No, the house is selling as-is. Any inspection is the oblig-ation of the buyer. I'd be happy to recommend a few people who do that work for us, but it's your responsibility to pay them." Her cell phone rang before she could finish.

Allie and I were left to marvel at all of the high-end appli-ances while Gloria stepped into the next room to take her call. I was checking out the faucet over the stove when she returned.

"It's for making pasta, so you don't have to carry the pot from the sink," she said, looking at me oddly. Her stiff posture was back, and now she was all business now. "I'm afraid we'll have to finish this later, Jake. I have to fill in for a colleague at her closing. She got stuck in Kansas City and is supposed to close on a house shortly."

"No problem, but I can't make an offer until I've checked out a few things. Would you mind if I come back with a ladder so I can at least take a closer look at the roof?"

She seemed to study me for a moment. "I suppose that won't hurt, but I will have to be here if you want to go inside." Her smile was back, along with a little gleam in her eyes.

· • • ●•●● • ·

Because we couldn't tell if Carl had taken anything or why he had gone to Madeline's house after Gloria had given us the quick tour of the house, I went back with Fred the day after meeting the realtor. Allie stayed behind to help Bonnie sort out her closets for a church rummage sale. Truth be told, I think the way Gloria acted had upset her, and she didn't want to see the house again.

"You let me know if anyone comes by to see what I'm up to, okay?" I said while setting up my ladder to reach the porch roof.

Fred waited long enough for me to climb the ladder before exploring the backyard once I was out of his sight. I might as well have brought Tigger for a lookout, at least she never pretended to help.

The wrap-around porch had a relatively flat roof that gave me access to the steeper roof of the house. It was worse than I'd thought. From the ground, it looked as if a few shingles had been blown off and would need replacing, but once I got a closer look, I saw they were too old and brittle to fix. From what I knew about roofing, it meant removing three layers of shingles that had been nailed down over the original wood shingles.

In the center of the main roof was a small gable with a window covered by shutters. Several of the shutter slats had broken away, allowing me to look inside. I used the flashlight of my phone to see a finished room with baby furniture covered in dust. The room must have been Stephanie's nursery when she was a baby.

Then it hit me.

What if Maddie's killer had hidden in the room until the coast was clear and left the way he had got in there? Was that even possible? I hadn't found an attic opening in the bedroom closet or anywhere else in the room when Bonnie and I pretended to be home inspectors. Up until now, I had assumed Maddie's murderer had left through the basement the way Fred had. I now wished that we had checked into the cellar door that led outside.

Access to the attic had to be from another room, through a trap door in the ceiling, or maybe a staircase. I realized that the best way to find it was in the attic itself, so I tried to see if the shutters would open.

There was a simple hook on the inside keeping them closed that I was able to lift with the blade of my pocket knife. Once I opened the shutters, I saw that the window was an old-style one where both panes slid open and could be locked with a latch in the center. The lock was in the open position so all I needed to do was slide the bottom pane up and climb inside. Unfortunately, it wasn't that simple. There were so many coats of paint on the jamb that the window was stuck closed. I needed another way in.

I finally looked up toward the peak of the gable and saw a vent with broken slats. The opening wasn't enough for a person to crawl through, assuming someone could reach it, but it was large enough for squirrels, birds, and Tigger, of course. That must have been how she got into the house. She had probably been chasing some critter. There had to be access from the attic to the rooms below if that was the way she got in, and I had to find that access.

I had two options: scrape away years of paint off the window or enter the house through the front door. The last choice would be the easiest, but either way could be considered breaking and entering. As I was damned either way, I chose the easy way.

Fred had returned from his exploration by the time I climbed off the ladder and walked up to the front door. He looked at me like Scooby-Doo does at Shaggy before doing something he shouldn't. I almost expected him to ask, What up?

After looking to see if I was being watched, I pulled my cell phone out of my pocket and tapped the video apps. It only took a few seconds to see the code Gloria had entered in the lockbox to get to the front door key.

"So, Freddie, which room do we try first?" I asked after Fred and I entered and shut the door behind us.

He took off down the hall leading toward the bedrooms. Fred turned around and barked at me with a huge smile on his face.

Chapter Twenty-two

FRED WAS SITTING IN front of a closet that had been converted into a space for laundry. A stackable washer/dryer was sitting in a recessed opening with bi-fold doors that were open. Fred had gone over to the washer to check it out with his nose. He'd taken one sniff before barking at me.

"Don't tell me you found something?" I said as I went over for a closer inspection, wondering why Maddie had two washing machines. I'd seen a newer, front-loading model in the basement when Bonnie and I had been there earlier. I reached down to rub the top of his head when I saw the washer hoses were not attached to anything. There weren't any faucets on the wall for them to connect to. "That's odd, Freddie, but what's even stranger are the grooves in the hardwood floor. It looks like this washer has been moved more than once. Is that what you are trying to tell me?"

I didn't wait for him to answer and grabbed the washer with both hands and tried to move it. To my surprise, it didn't take much effort. It slid to the side along the wall as if it were on wheels. That's when I saw what had made the marks on the floor. The washer *was* on wheels, or small rollers, to be precise. And behind the washer was an opening no higher than the washer that had been hiding it. This must have been the entrance to the attic before someone removed the door and its casings, converting the space to look like a laundry closet.

I had to duck to get through the opening but was able to stand once I was on the other side of the wall, and saw stairs leading to the attic. Fred didn't have that problem and followed me in. An old light switch, the kind with buttons for on and off instead of the newer toggle switch, was on the wall at the base of the stairs. Hoping that no one had turned off the power since I'd flipped the main breaker, I pushed the top button, and a light at the top of the stairs went on. We went up and into the finished room I had seen through the shutters.

I pushed another old-style light switch at the top of the stairs that turned on an ornate ceiling fixture and illuminated the room. A quick look confirmed what I'd seen through the shutters and a lot more. In addition to the crib and rocking chair, there was a desk with a computer on the same wall as the window. I suppose that's why I hadn't seen it and assumed the room was a nursery. It was close enough to the window to let whoever sat there have a view of the driveway and road through the broken slats of the shutters.

The desk furniture had to have been a recent addition. Unlike the baby furniture, the desk was made of cheap pressed board, something from Walmart or Target; whereas, the baby furniture was old and expensive. I wasn't an expert on antiques, but I knew the rocker had to be at least one hundred years old. It looked handmade and had little cherubs or angels carved into its arms and seat back. Aside from the dust covering it, it looked as good as the day it had been made.

I let my eyes drift from the chair to the crib. The tiny mattress was covered by a faded pink blanket. It looked as if it hadn't been used in a long time. I walked over to the dresser next to the crib and opened the top draw but not before noticing a pair of pictures on top of the dresser. One of the pictures was of a young couple and their baby at her christening. The child was crying from the water the priest had used to baptize her with. The other picture saw the couple kneeling at a headstone in the church cemetery. I couldn't read the headstone in the picture, but I knew it could be important, so I took a picture of the photograph with my cell phone, hoping I'd be able to zoom in on it later.

Someone had been using the space as a home office, yet they hadn't removed the baby furniture. Could the picture be a clue into that person's mind? Maybe I'd find more by looking at the computer. I figured it wasn't password protected as it was already in a hidden office slash nursery, and I was right. After powering it on, I decided to click on a Facebook icon in the taskbar tray. That account was password protected and gave me no clue who had been using it as the last user had logged out and deleted all traces of a username and password.

Next, I decided to check their browsing history and discovered that someone had been searching for ancestry sites. I tried a couple of the pages they had visited and found they'd created an account on Ancestery.com under the username Born2Fish. Again, they had not saved the password, so I couldn't find who it was. What I did find, though, when I checked their web browsing history, was that they visited a locksmith's page and a supplier of welding gasses.

I was about to check out those pages when Fred barked from the lower level. I hadn't noticed him go back downstairs. A quick glance out the window told me we had company. I quickly closed the dresser drawer, ran down the stairs, and barely had time to move the washing machine back in place when I heard the front door open.

Gloria was standing just inside the front door, clutching her purse to her chest. "Mr. Martin? What are you doing here?

And how did you get in?" she asked as I strolled into the living room.

"Hi, Gloria. The roof is so bad, I thought I'd better check if it was leaking inside. I was going to call you, but when I saw the door was unlocked, I decided not to bother you. I hope you don't mind."

She was slow to respond. "I wish you had asked permission. I could get into a lot of trouble having a client roam free in a listing," she said after a hard swallow and looking around the room.

"You could always tell them you asked me to check for leaks, which by the way, I didn't find any. That alone is a miracle considering the shape of your roof." Once more, I found myself babbling on, but before I could put my foot any further into my mouth, someone else came up the stairs and into the house.

"What a beautiful dog. Does he come with the house?" A woman who looked to be in her early forties with dark hair cut like a boy bent down to pet Fred on the head.

Gloria forced a smile at the woman's joke. "I'm sorry, Christi. I thought he'd be gone before I showed you the house. I asked Mr. Martin to check the roof to see if it was leaking." She looked at me, no longer forcing a smile. "Please send me your inspection report, Jake, I'll need to show it to whoever buys the house."

Christi stopped petting Fred and looked up at me. She had piercing hazel eyes that made me feel as if she had seen through Gloria's lie. "Does he climb ladders to help you on the roof, too?" she asked.

"Not yet. We're working on that, though." I gave a small laugh, hoping someone would change the subject.

She leaned forward and held out her hand. "Well, I may need a roofer if I buy the house. Do you have a card, Mr. Martin?"

"Um, no, and please, call me Jake. I'm sorry if I gave you the impression I did roofing. I was inspecting it for myself. I've been thinking about buying an old house to fix up and resell," I said, shaking her hand. Her grip surprised me. Not only did it feel like I had my hand in a vice, but I also felt her callouses.

"If I didn't already have a partner, Jake, I'd suggest we join forces. We flip houses, too. But the offer still stands; roofing is the one thing I won't do. Heights scare me to death."

"If your partner isn't afraid of heights, and you don't go with metal, he ought to be able to handle it."

She let out a small yelp and covered her mouth. "You're funny. My dad doesn't do anything besides put up the money I need for renovations."

Fred had decided to go outside once he saw he wasn't going to get any more head scratches. I could see that Gloria was getting impatient, too. She kept glancing at her wristwatch as if she had to be somewhere else. "Like I said, Jake, send your report to my office. Now, Christi, why don't I show you the kitchen? The previous owner did a wonderful job remodeling it. I'm sure you'll approve."

Christi sighed as I headed for the door. "I'd rather see the basement first, if you don't mind," I heard her say as I left to find my dog.

I caught up with Fred down the driveway, his nose was smelling Gloria's Escalade.

"Yeah, I know. She could feed all the dogs in the state for what that rig cost, but we have better things to do than check out the new car smell. Get in the truck, will you? I need to find the cemetery in that photo."

Chapter Twenty-three

I GOT A TEXT from Allie when Fred and I were on our way home. She said she and Bonnie were going shopping in Sedalia and wouldn't be back until later. I suppose they got bored sorting clothes for the church rummage sale or decided to replace the ones they were giving away with new clothes. Either way, it looked like I'd have a little quiet time to search the Internet to see where the cemetery was that I saw in the photo.

Unfortunately, I'd taken my eyes off the road a little too long, and a small deer had decided to cross the road while I was looking at my phone. Fred's bark made me look up, but it was too late. His bark made the deer turn back and run into the rear of my truck. I stopped to move the deer off the road and was startled when it got up and ran into the woods as I approached it. It was okay and only stunned. My truck was another matter.

The deer had made a dent in the side of the bed when it hit the truck.

Once we were back at our little home, I fed Fred some of his dry dog food and gave him fresh water. He stuck up his nose at the dog food and went straight for the water, where he got more on the floor than he drank. I laughed and pulled out my phone to see if I could zoom in on the picture I'd taken of the photograph in the hidden room. I didn't have any luck with my phone as it became too pixelated when I tried zooming in so, I downloaded it to my computer where I could use a more sophisticated photo editor.

With the help of a good photo editor, I saw that the gravestone marker was, as I suspected, for a baby girl, whose name was Ashley Monroe, born on October 26th, 1976, and died on October 31st, 1980. I decided to see what I could find about Ashley on the web, but when I brought up a web browser, I realized I had no idea what to look for. I'd ask Fred, but he'd gone outside to play with Tigger so I was on my own. It was just as well. He'd probably lead me to pet cemeteries spelled with a capital S like in the book by Stephen King.

I did, however, discover that most cemeteries had a list with the location of where people were resting. Resting was the word the first site used. I always found it strange that someone is put to rest when they are buried. Do dead people really rest? Anyway, I searched several sites looking for Ashley Monroe. I found a lot of Monroes and a few named Ashley, but the ones I found were all over seventy.

I was getting frustrated and decided to take another approach. One of my searches made that decision for me when Madeline Monroe's name popped up in a Clark County, Nevada, vital statistics database. When I clicked on the link, it showed a marriage certificate from the late seventies. On a hunch, I typed in "birth certificate" and "Madeline Monroe" and found that she'd had twins, Ashley and Amber, in Sedalia, Missouri. I also discovered that Madeline divorced her husband, Robert, less than a year after the date on the tombstone in the photograph.

I was writing down that the photo I found in the nursery probably belonged to Maddie when Fred started barking from outside. I closed my web browser and went to see what he was barking at.

· · · · ● ● · ● · · ·

"So, Maddie had twins?" Bonnie asked after I'd carried in bags of groceries and some clothes she and Allie had bought in Sedalia. We were sitting at her kitchen table, waiting for my reward of fresh coffee while munching on an oatmeal cookie. Allie had already gone to her room to try on her new outfit.

Bonnie was hovering over the coffee pot as if watching it would make it finish sooner.

"That's what the birth certificate says," I answered, dropping Fred a bite of the cookie I was eating when Bonnie had her back turned to pour us some coffee.

She returned to the table, smiled at Fred, then looked at me and shook her head. "And you think the other twin died shortly after being born?"

"The date on the grave stone is less than a week after the date on the birth certificate. And the names match, so I'd say yes.

"I suppose it's why they divorced. One of them must have blamed the other for the baby dying." She had a vacant look in her eyes and I don't think she was debating whether to fortify her coffee. "Is Stephanie the twin who survived?"

"No. The surviving twin was named Amber. Stephanie must be in her early thirties; Amber was at least ten years older."

Bonnie pulled out the pot from her coffee maker before it was finished to fill my cup. "Wow, that poor woman, losing two baby girls. No wonder she committed suicide," she said, handing me my coffee.

I felt like saying something like my cup of coffee was going to be too strong but let it go. "If it was suicide. Anyway, Amber died before social media was popular so I didn't find much on her. I think Kelly might have better luck. She has access to records that I don't."

Bonnie went back and poured herself a cup before sitting down across from me at the table. "I'm glad she's back to work. Did she say if she still wants the job with the Highway Patrol?"

"No. The last I talked to her, she had to cut it short to stop her mother from doing something. She yelled something to her, then said she'd call me back before hanging up the phone." I hadn't taken a sip of my coffee because I knew it would be too strong, but there was no way I was going to suggest switching cups with her because she had doctored hers with milk and several spoons of sugar.

Bonnie looked up from her coffee before breaking off a piece of cookie and giving it to Goldie, who must have smelled the cookie I'd been eating and left Allie to dress herself. "Alzheimer's can do funny things to people. Does she still recognize Kelly?"

"I thought you said that people food wasn't good for them. Are you a dog murderer now?" I laughed, not at her question about Kelly's mother but because of the irony of her feeding Goldie.

"Of course not. I don't want it to go to waste. Besides, Tigger would just turn up her nose at it, and goldens will eat anything."

"Ain't that the truth," I said after Goldie downed the cookie in record time and begged for more, "but you won't be so forgiving when I tell you why I won't be able to use my truck to move the stuff you wanted me to take to the rummage sale today."

Bonnie blinked and her eyebrows drew closer together. "Did you get in an accident or something?"

"Nothing serious, Bon. We startled a small buck grazing on our way back from Maddie's house. Fred barked and the buck took off, running into my truck. I'm afraid there's a dent in the bed and now I can't get the tailgate closed. Your stuff might fall out if I hit a bump or hill."

Her hand shot to her mouth as though she'd eaten something terrible. "Is the deer okay?"

"He's fine. A little stunned at first, but he ran off into the woods as if nothing happened. Unfortunately, I can't say the same for my truck."

"I don't care about the stupid rummage sale as long as he's okay," Bonnie said.

"I'm sure he's okay. I'll take my truck to the body shop tomorrow. I'll let Clyde try to remove the dent using dry ice, so maybe he won't have to sand and paint it."

Her eyes softened, and a slow smile formed on her lips. "Don't bother, Jake. I'll use my Jeep for the boxes of clothes. We'll donate the furniture next time."

I pushed my nearly full coffee cup forward and rose out of my chair. "It's no bother and thanks for the coffee and cookies. They were delicious.

"I'll take my truck in tomorrow. Maybe Clyde will fix it in time to move your stuff. In the meantime, Fred and I have some sleuthing to do. Maybe we can find an obituary or something that will give us more information on Maddie's daughter."

I saw Bonnie frown when she noticed I hadn't taken more than a sip of her coffee, so I decided to tell a little white lie. "Sorry I didn't drink the coffee. My stomach has been upset lately, and caffeine might make it worse." I yelled, "Bye," to my daughter, who was still trying on her new outfits, and walked over to my little house to begin searching the Internet before Bonnie could ask if I wanted to try one of her home remedies or ask about Kelly again.

The last I'd heard from Kelly, she was thinking about taking more leave so she could take her mother on a cruise. I wanted to go with her, but she said she needed time alone with her mother before Alzheimer's got to her. Bonnie didn't need to know any of that, and I didn't need any snake oil.

• • • • • • • • •

My Internet search for obituaries got me nowhere. Fred wasn't much help, either. His restless sleep at my feet wouldn't let me concentrate. He kept kicking his feet like he was running after something, and every so often, I could see his eyes move up and down under closed lids. Either he was still chasing the deer who'd run into my truck, or he had indeed, eaten too much.

I found myself searching YouTube for videos on paint-less dent repair when I didn't get anywhere with the obit search. The first couple of videos showed do-it-yourselfers trying to remove hail dents. They used a combination of heat and rapid cooling with compressed gas from a spray can. Neither guy was successful. I finally saw a clip where a pro managed to remove a larger dent with persuasion from a rubber hammer after using a heat gun, followed by spreading dry ice pellets on the dented surface. This guy had to wear special gloves, so he didn't burn himself with the pellets. That's how he described the freezing of his skin. The irony of burning oneself with ice made me smile. It was enough, however, to make me realize that it was a job best left to professionals.

I finally gave up both my searches when Fred woke, and I decided to call Kelly before going to bed.

"Hope I didn't catch you at a bad time." It dawned on me how pathetic I must have sounded.

"No. Mom's sound asleep. I fell asleep in the chair myself."
I could hear the soft sounds of a television in the background.
It sounded like Rick Steves in one of his travel shows.

"Have you decided where you guys are going?"

"I thought I told you. The home in Lincoln will take her
social security and the small pension my father left her." Her
tone no longer sounded sleepy, but short.

"No, I meant on the cruise. I'd still love to go with you.
Bonnie will watch Fred and I can get my own cabin if that's
a problem."

She sighed deeply. "She'll forget who I am in a couple of
months so please, Jake, I need this time alone with her alone."
I decided not to update her on what I had found at Maddie's.
It was obvious her hands were full, caring for her mother.

Chapter Twenty-four

ALLIE DIDN'T HAVE ANYTHING special planned for the day, so I talked her into going with Fred and me to the body shop. Even if they weren't successful in removing the dent in my truck, I'd have Clyde fix it so I'd be able to close my tailgate and help Bonnie move her furniture for the rummage sale.

"We studied the change of state for various materials in chemistry last semester. That must be why they use dry ice to remove those dents," she said as I explained how paint-less dent removal was done.

I tried not to hide the smile I felt forming on my face. Never in a thousand years would I have thought my own daughter would show an interest in science.

"It's the change of temperature caused when the carbon dioxide changes from a solid to a gas. It's one of the few compounds that goes directly from a solid to a gas without a liquid state. I suppose that's why they use it."

My expression turned from one of pride to curiosity. "I don't follow, Allie. What does skipping the liquid stage have to do with removing dents?"

She laughed and gave me the explain-it-to-old-people look. "It's not as messy. If you notice, there's nothing to clean up after the dry ice sublimates."

I hesitated for a second at her vocabulary. Evidently, I hesitated too long.

"Changes from a solid to a gas," she added.

"I know what sublimate means, smarty. I was just surprised to hear you say it."

Fred interrupted our father-daughter moment by barking. Johnny, Clyde's body repairman, had quit working on the dent and was coming toward us.

"The dent was too big. I guess it ain't gonna work."

"I didn't think freezing a dent that size would work. Something that big isn't very malleable or ductile as a small dent, but at least it didn't leave a mess when it sublimated," Allie said to no one in particular.

Johnny looked at her as if she'd just announced Jesus' second coming. "It don't hurt none to give it a try, anyway. Where'd you learn all them ten-dollar words, missy?'

"She was a chemistry major," I said. "I think what she's trying to tell us is that I need a new tailgate."

Allie pretended to pout while looking down at Fred. "You understand me, don't you, Freddie?"

He barked and smiled at the attention.

I would have smiled, but I had a sudden epiphany. "Of course, that's how he did it."

Johnny tilted his head to the side and tugged at his right earlobe.

"Come on, Allie. I need to call Kelly," I said before turning back to Johnny. "How much do I owe you for trying to remove those dents?"

"I can't charge you for something I didn't do. I learned a bunch of new words I might use on the next customer, so we'll call it even, bud."

I reached into my wallet, pulled out a twenty, and handed it to him. "At least let me pay you for your time. You may have helped in more ways than you'll ever know."

· · · · •·•·•·· ·

"What was all that about?" Allie asked once we were on our way back home. Her eyes were as piercing as her mother's had been so many years ago when she'd ask me a question I didn't want to answer. She even reminded me of Natalie in better times. Neither one would ever be on the cover of the latest beauty magazine--they weren't skinny enough--but that's what I had loved about Natalie.

"Your statement that dry ice doesn't leave a mess. That and the fact I remembered from my chemistry classes that it also replaces the oxygen around it when it melts."

She rolled her eyes and crossed her arms. "Sublimates," she said, pretending an air of superiority.

"The point is, my dear, it explains why Bonnie and I found all those dead bugs by the highboy. Bugs die without oxygen. Someone used blocks of dry ice to make the highboy tip over and block the door after they'd killed Maddie and left the room."

Allie tilted her head to one side. "But both sides would have sublimated at the same rate, unless..." She took a deep breath. "No, that doesn't make sense either."

"What doesn't make sense?" I asked, scratching my head.

Allie's posture stiffened, then drooped. "I was thinking he used the heater to make one side melt faster than the other, but didn't you say the power had been turned off?"

"You're a chip off the old block, Sherlock. That's how he did it. The power had been shut off at the breaker box, not at the pole. He must have turned on the power and come in later to flip the main breaker back off."

Allie grinned

. "You mean Irene, don't you? The woman Sherlock fell for?"

"Maybe on TV."

"Whatever, Dad. I'm just glad I could help," she said. "So, what's next? Are you going to ask Kelly to check local dry ice vendors to see if any of our suspects have made a purchase recently?"

It was a good thing I was driving and not looking at Allie or she might have noticed my bitter smile. "We need to solve this ourselves and not involve Kelly. She has her hands full right now."

"Because of Sheriff Bennett and Detective Teller?" she asked. I noticed her voice had softened.

I simply nodded my head, "Well, it looks like you're learning something up at that college after all. I would have never put all the pieces together without your insight," I said, trying to change the subject.

Chapter Twenty-five

"THEY COULD HAVE BEEN in a freezer for months before he used them," Bonnie said after Allie after I went over my theory about how the high-boy had been tipped over while sitting at Bonnie's kitchen table.

Allie leaned back in her chair and ran her fingers through her hair. "The temperature of home freezers isn't cold enough. It would have sublimated before he could use it."

Bonnie looked over at my daughter. I could see she wanted to say something but couldn't find the words. "It needs to be stored below one hundred and ten degrees. Home freezers don't get that cold," Allie said before Bonnie could speak.

"Which is why we need to check all the dry ice vendors in the area to see who might have bought some blocks of the stuff right before Maddie was murdered," I said.

"I can do that," Allie replied. She was grinning and had a gleam in her eyes I hadn't seen in a long time. It was obvious Allie enjoyed helping solve the murders, but as a father, I had to worry about her involvement if she got too close to the murderer. "I don't want you to call them, Allie. I'll ask Kelly to make the calls after I tell her how I think the highboy was tipped over to block the door. She will have better luck with that than we could."

Allie shrugged and tilted her head to the side. "I thought you said you didn't want to involve Kelly because she had her hands full." My daughter caught me off guard, again, and I hesitated to answer.

"I could do it," Bonnie answered while taking a seat at the table. She had been too nervous to sit after Allie had shot down her theory about storing dry ice and had kept herself busy feeding the dogs. She said it with both of her elbows on the table so she could hold her head in her hands while waiting for me to say something.

"No. It would be too dangerous if the killer thinks one of you is snooping around. We'll let Kelly handle it."

Bonnie winced and showed her frustration by shaking her head. "You've put me in more dangerous situations than this before," she said, pouting.

"Sorry, Bon, but the dry ice vendors are more likely to respond to a sheriff's deputy than any of us. It will also help her look like she's a better detective than Teller."

"She won't even return your calls. What makes you think she cares enough to call all the businesses that sell dry ice?" Bonnie had dropped her arms and sat back in her chair, crossing her arms across her chest.

She was right, as usual. The chances of Kelly agreeing to check out the dry ice vendors was slim at best. I needed a back-up plan that didn't involve Bonnie or my daughter. "Maybe I can find something online without alerting anyone," I replied, knowing I had no idea how I would do it.

My daughter grabbed my arm tightly. "I'll ask Aadesh if he can hack into their databases," she said, grinning widely.

"Aadesh?" Bonnie asked.

"He's the resident geek in our dorm. He was hitting on me all last semester, so I'm sure he'll be happy to help."

"Aren't we putting the cart before the horse?" Bonnie asked, shaking her head again. "Before we ask anyone for help, I think we need to get a list of suspects so Aadesh, or whoever contacts the vendors, has some idea who might have bought the dry ice."

I simply nodded my head in agreement. "And try to connect them to our list of suspects." Bonnie was so excited that I didn't want to ruin the moment for her by telling her I'd already thought of cross-referencing buyers to our suspects, so I made it look like her idea.

She got up, went to her junk drawer, and came back shortly with a notepad. "Here's the list of suspects I wrote down a while back."

"First on your list is the developer we thought bribed the commissioners," I said after a quick glance at the list.

Allie wrinkled her brow. Her expression made me think she might be having second thoughts about asking her friend for help. "Should I ask Aadesh to search each vendor's sales to see if anyone on that list bought dry ice before the murder?"

"That might take too long. The longer he stays connected to their systems, the greater is the chance he'll be caught. No, I think if he can simply get us a list of their dry ice sales, I can put that data in a database and write a SQL program to cross-reference it with our suspect list. It will minimize his hacking time and keep the suspect list to ourselves. There's no need to let him know any more than is necessary."

Allie frowned, and I noticed her jaw going slack, so I continued, "Next is Maddie's daughter and her husband. They have the most to gain, which gives them the best motive."

Bonnie leaned forward, licking her lips. "Maybe they're in it with the redneck who drove me off the road."

"He's on the list next to Stephanie," I answered. "Carl is definitely involved. I just don't know how yet."

Allie's frown had been replaced with a wrinkled brow as she pointed to Carl's name on my list. "And his uncle. He's hiding something. I think it's more than protecting his nephew," she said in a steady, low-pitched voice.

I added "Carl's uncle" to my list and looked up. "Anyone else?"

"We still can't rule out the sheriff and his affair with Maddie," Bonnie said. She had gone back to fussing with her cat after feeding the dogs. Tigger had been trying to get her attention by winding through Bonnie's legs as if they were some kind of scratching posts.

"He's already on the list," I said, pointing to his name.

"Good. If that affair became public knowledge, it could ruin his chance of being re-elected." She stopped petting Tigger and sat back in her chair, crossing her arms again.

"And let's not forget Deputy Teller," I said, adding him to our list. "He was up to something when he met with Carl at the docks. Maybe he paid Carl to do it before Maddie went public with her affair with Bennett. He is the sheriff's favorite nephew, after all." It was probably wishful thinking on my part, as he would definitely lose his job if convicted and make an opening for Kelly.

Bonnie waved her hands wildly. "And don't forget the phony suicide text he sent," she said.

"But why would he have the other commissioner killed?" Allie asked. She shook her head and continued, "No, my money's on the developer. It had to be someone with a reason or grudge against the commissioners."

"Morgan could have been blackmailing Bennett," Bonnie said. Her eyes were focused on her cat, suggesting the doubt in her statement; Tigger was now in Bonnie's lap, purring.

I put a question mark next to Bennett and Detective Teller. "Duly noted, but I don't think we need to spend much time on either of them, at least not for the murders. Teller is up to something but that's something we can check into after we find out who killed the commissioners."

I put down my pen and looked up. "I think we have enough suspects, for now...unless you two can think of someone else who had motive, means, and opportunity to kill the commissioners."

Allie glanced at Bonnie, then focused her attention on me. "What about Maddie's husband? Maybe he found out about her affairs and killed her in a fit of rage."

"That does give him a motive, but he hasn't been around for a while, so I don't see any means or opportunity. I'll add him to the bottom of the list just in case, though," I said, returning to my notepad.

NOTHING TO DIE FOR

Allie shook her head. "I was thinking about her first husband. Maybe he still blamed Maddie for the death of their baby."

I'd forgotten all about Maddie's first husband and wondered if he hated her enough to kill her. "Why would he seek revenge after all these years?" I asked. "I'll add him to our list but unless my search shows him buying some dry ice, I don't think we need to waste any time on him."

"Speaking of dry ice, I can get that list of CO_2 vendors for your database. I'll ask Siri for all the places in the area that sell dry ice," Allie said, getting up from her chair. "I'll go get it now."

"And the file from your friend?" Bonnie asked.

I held up my hand to signal Allie to stop. "On second thought, let's not get Aadesh involved. Hacking is illegal,l and I wouldn't be able to sleep nights if he got caught. I need to think of another way to find who bought dry ice before Maddie's murder. However, making a list of vendors isn't illegal, so why don't you do that, Allie, while I check out our suspect list?" Maybe I was going at this the wrong way. Instead of looking for a connection between vendors and my suspects, I should be asking myself who on my suspect list used or needed dry ice.

. . . .

I returned to our suspect list after I'd gone home and given Fred his dinner, or, as is usually the case, he finished my dinner. I'd warmed up some leftover meatloaf that Bonnie had given me a few days ago. Fred didn't seem to mind as he gobbled it down in a couple of bites without tasting it. He was now sound asleep at my feet while I concentrated on doing some Internet searching.

Whoever thought of using the dry ice had to be familiar with it. They had to know it would melt without leaving a trace, which meant they'd either used it or were some kind of science nerd.

I could probably eliminate Carl, the redneck. He didn't seem like the kind of person who would be interested in science. True, he might have been employed at a body shop at one time or some manufacturing job where they used dry ice pellets instead of sand as an abrasive, but from what I heard of his work record, I didn't think so. The two people with the most to gain from bumping off Maddie were her daughter and husband. I'd have to look into them closer.

Maddie's daughter, Stephanie, made my search easy as she had both a Facebook and a Twitter account she used regularly. Her "About" page on Facebook said she was a former fifth-grade teacher. I wasn't as lucky finding information on her husband, but Stephanie did mention in one of her posts that he got a job recently, driving for a medical supply company. I assumed he'd have access to dry ice as it is used to transport organs and certain medicines so I used that to narrow down my search. I found a Steven Travers who worked for an organ transport service in Excelsior Springs.

The only thing I found on Steven was in Missouri's Casenet records, an online database for most court cases in every county in Missouri. Other than several entries in Casenet for traffic violations and one DUI, I couldn't find anything else about him online. The guy was a ghost when it came to social media. He didn't even have a Facebook account, and I decided my effort was probably better spent concentrating on Stephanie. Fifth-grade teachers must know about the properties of dry ice because it is used in plenty of elementary science experiments.

The thought of involving Allie's friend in an illegal hack bothered me. It was beginning to look as if I'd have to hack the vendors myself if I was going to identify the person who had bought the dry ice to knock over Maddie's highboy. I could use a virtual private network to mask my IP address when I logged into the vendor's computer, but I was paranoid because I didn't know if the VPN provider would be able to trace the hack to my computer.

The safest way for me to hide my identity was to use someone else's network and computer, someone who had no idea their router had been used in an illegal search. I finally decided to buy a laptop off of craigslist for cash and to use a public network, so if my hacking was discovered, it would be nearly impossible to trace it to me.

· · · · ●· ● · · ·

"What if they trace the computer to the craigslist seller, and he or she identifies you?" Bonnie asked as Allie and I sat at her kitchen table the next day. She had corralled me into joining them for lunch when I told her about my plan. It seemed Bonnie's paranoia was greater than mine, or maybe she simply read more thrillers about conspiracy theories than I did.

I pinched off a piece of the salami sandwich Bonnie had made and gave it to Fred, who hadn't taken his eyes off it since Bonnie made it. "It's not like I'm hacking into the CIA's computers. I doubt if Bennett or any other local cop would bother to try and find me, assuming they even discover my intrusion."

Bonnie rolled her eyes.

"What? Do you know something I don't?"

"You keep doing that, and he will never leave you alone."

"But getting back to finding who bought the dry ice, what will you do with the information if you do find it? You can't go to Kelly with it; she will want to know how you got it."

She had me there. I'd been so excited about my theory of how the killer had managed to tip over the highboy that I hadn't thought that far ahead. "I'll cross that bridge when I get to it," I said, tossing Fred the rest of my sandwich. Bonnie had ruined my appetite.

"Dad can always tell her he found a receipt in the suspect's trash or something." Allie had kept quiet only because, as I saw out of the corner of my eye, she'd been sneaking Goldie part of her sandwich.

Fred left my side and went over to my daughter. My sandwich was gone, and he must have seen her feed Goldie. "Aren't we getting ahead of ourselves?" I asked. "Let's worry about what to do with the information if and when we get it." I got up from the table and called my fairweather friend. "Come on, Freddy. We have to find us a computer so I can commit a felony."

· · · · ● · ● · · ·

Fred and I were back on the road within an hour. I'd found the perfect laptop in Warrensburg using Facebook Marketplace. I only knew the seller as Carrie, a name I'd seen on her listing. We agreed to meet at her storage shed in ninety minutes. Her husband was a mechanic for the Air Force and was currently deployed overseas. She was selling off their unwanted computer equipment in preparation for their next move once he returned. Unlike professional vendors online, I doubted if they even bothered to reformat the hard drive or delete the browser's cookies and history. Then, I saw that their computer still had its hard drive and operating system. It was perfect.

I parked outside the gate and away from the security cameras and picked up my cell phone. I didn't want the cameras or the woman I was meeting to get a picture of my truck or license number. "Hi, Carrie," I said once I punched in her number. "I'm at your storage facility, outside the main gate."

Before I could hang up, someone knocked on my window, and I nearly dropped my phone. I'd been so engrossed in the phone call I failed to see the young woman approach my truck, and Fred hadn't barked out a warning as he had been sleeping next to me, oblivious to the fact that he was supposed to be my lookout.

"Jake Martin?" she asked.

I looked up from my phone into squinting blue eyes and a young woman with a wrinkled forehead. "Carrie?" I answered, at a loss for words, wondering how she knew my name.

"I thought it was you. You look just like the picture on your Facebook profile. And then I saw your golden asleep on the seat and knew it had to be you."

"You checked my Facebook page?"

She smiled and looked me in the eyes. "A girl can't be too careful these days. Anyway, I hope this will get you back to writing. I loved your last book and can't wait for the next one," she said, holding up a notebook PC for me to see.

· · · · ●· ● · · · ·

"So much for buying a PC that can't be traced," I said to Fred as I drove back onto US 50.

He tilted his head to the side and looked at me as if I'd lost it. Maybe I had, for I ended up buying the computer even though I knew I couldn't use it as planned. I would have to think of another way to hack the dry ice databases now that the computer could easily be traced back to me, but first I needed the list of dry ice vendors my daughter said she'd get.

Chapter Twenty-six

I DIDN'T HAVE TO wait long. Fred's bark woke me the next morning. I got out of bed and threw on my robe just in time.

"Dad, are you up yet?"

"I am now. What time is it anyway?"

"I couldn't wait any longer. I asked Siri for a list of dry ice vendors near us and thought you'd like to see them."

I waved Allie toward the table that served as both my kitchen and dining table while I went to the counter to make coffee. I couldn't function this early without it. "Siri? Wouldn't it have been easier to use a computer to print a list?" I asked after filling the coffee machine with water and adding grounds to the drip basket.

"No, but I can send you the list if you need a digital copy." She let her thumbs dance on her phone's screen for a few seconds, then looked up at me, smiling. "Done. Check your email. I just sent you an attachment you can use for your database. I'll start breakfast while you check it out."

I wasn't quite ready to get back to work after being up half the night but Fred and Goldie had gone out, so I couldn't make the excuse that I had to let him out. I did as I was told, sat down at the table, and booted the laptop I'd bought in Warrensburg. " Let me get out of my bathrobe while this antique boots," I said and headed for the bedroom.

"How do you want your eggs?" I heard my daughter ask through my thin walls as I was going through my hamper for the cleanest dirty jeans I could find.

"Cooked," I replied. "However you like them is fine with me."

I emerged from my bedroom five minutes later. I had found a pair of jeans with only a stain on the knees from when I'd bent down outside to tie my shoelace when I'd been checking my truck's tire pressure. Fortunately for Allie, I also found a clean undershirt and some deodorant, before joining her at my table. My shower would have to wait.

"Wow! That's a lot of vendors," I said after looking at Allie's list, taking a cautionary bite of scrambled eggs. I knew she hadn't learned to cook from her mother, Natalie couldn't boil water, so I didn't know if they would be cooked through.

"Who would have thought you could buy dry ice in so many places."

Fred came back inside while I was looking at the list. "Did you smell the eggs?" I asked, petting him on the head.

He ignored the eggs and barked at me.

"Where's Goldie, Freddie?" my daughter asked, cutting me off before I could ask Fred if he wanted a bite. I could see by the worry lines on her forehead that she was concerned that Goldie hadn't returned with Fred.

Fred ran to the door and barked before scooting through his doggy door when he saw me get out of my chair. I knew something had to be wrong when he ignored a handout.

"Goldie--come here, girl," Allie called from my porch after running after Fred and me. He had taken off toward Bonnie's barn, and I was not far behind.

"What the...," I started to say something and bit my tongue when I heard my daughter come up behind me. Allie ran past me to her dog who was lying next to my tractor.

Goldie tried to get up but cried out when she stood and fell back down. I went over to her and tried to comfort her by stroking her head. "What's wrong, girl?"

She looked at me with sad brown eyes and I could see she was in a lot of pain.

"We need to get her to the vet, Dad," Allie said between sobs.

I reached down and gently lifted her up. "Can you grab my keys off the hook and meet me at my truck?"

Allie stopped crying, wiped her tears, and ran out of the barn.

"Who did this to her, Freddie?" I asked after gently placing Goldie in my truck's backseat.

Fred ignored me, jumped into the seat next to Goldie, and laid his head down by her. Were those actual tears in his eyes, or was I imagining them? My mind was already working on the answer to my question. Was it someone who was simply looking for something to steal, or were they trying to leave us a message? I didn't have a security camera in the barn, but I did have one pointing to the driveway. However, it didn't always work as it was solar-powered. I made a mental note to check it later after we took Goldie to the vet.

· · · · ● · ● · · · ·

Dr. Steadman opened his mouth to speak, then paused as if weighing what he had to say. "It's a good thing you brought her in when you did," he said softly. "She had internal bleeding that we were able to stop. She would have bled out if you had waited."

Allie nodded hesitantly and cleared her throat. "Will she be okay?"

"Should be as good as new in a few weeks."

Allie let out a huge breath, and tears welled up in her eyes.

"We can thank Fred for that," Bonnie said. She had seen Allie run toward my house when I'd sent her to get the keys to my truck and realized something was wrong. After seeing Goldie lying in the backseat of my truck, she insisted on driving us to the vet's in her Jeep so I could keep Fred away from my daughter with Goldie in her arms.

"Any idea what caused the bleeding, Doc?" Bonnie asked.

Dr. Steadman's looked as if he'd survived a staring contest with Medusa, and barely at that. "If I had to hazard a guess, I'd say she'd been kicked."

Bonnie's mouth fell open. "Who would do that? The answer must have come to her before anyone could answer because she froze and took a step back. "She must have surprised someone in the barn."

"I'll bet it's that redneck, Dad." Allie's nostrils flared. "He must have kicked her to get even with us."

Dr. Steadman held a finger to his face. "Redneck describes half the county. What did you guys do to make somebody so mad at you that they took it out on your dog?" he asked.

"Are you sure someone kicked her? Could she have run into something? I mean, if someone was in the barn, Fred would have barked his head off," I said when I saw the concern in the good doctor's face. I didn't want to tell him about our encounter with Carl and his uncle or why Allie suspected him.

"I suppose that's possible if she had been chasing a cat or some other critter," Dr. Steadman answered, scratching the week-old stubble on his chin. "Anyway, like I said, she should be okay in a few weeks. Just make sure she doesn't chase anything else for a while."

"Thanks, Doc," I said and grabbed Bonnie by the elbow to lead her out before she could say any more about Carl. "I'm sure my daughter will watch her like a mother hen," I added before ushering everyone outside.

***

"Why the bum's rush?" Bonnie asked after we were on the road.

"I wasn't sure if the good doctor had to report animal abuse or not, and there was no need to find out," I said, thanking my decision to drive, so I didn't have to look Bonnie in the eyes.

I could see, out the side of my eye, Bonnie loosen up. I also saw my daughter nodding in the rear-view mirror, with Goldie in her lap. "You're right, Jake," Bonnie answered. "We don't need to hang our dirty laundry in front of strangers. We shouldn't have said anything about Carl in front of the doctor."

I simply nodded my head without looking at her. Thinking out loud in front of Bonnie usually raised more questions than answers, and now I had my daughter to worry about, too. I knew we must be getting close to whoever killed Maddie, but I doubted it was Carl. He just didn't seem smart enough to stage a suicide. Besides, why now? If it was Carl, wouldn't he have struck after our little incident with his truck?

"No, I don't think it was Carl. I'd say someone was sending us a message to back off, but outside of the three of us, nobody knew of my plan to check out dry ice vendors. Maybe it's not even related to the murders. Someone could have been looking for something to steal and the dogs surprised them," I said after a few seconds, pausing to think. I'd learned to think before talking to Bonnie.

"I still think it was the redneck, and I think he's in it with Maddie's daughter," Bonnie said, glancing at Goldie. We had left the highway for our narrow country road, so I knew I couldn't look at her, but I knew she was serious. She was convinced it was Carl.

"Or maybe one of our other suspects, like Maddie's husband or the developer. We haven't eliminated them from our suspect list," I answered.

"Why would they break into Bonnie's barn and kick Goldie?" Allie asked without looking up from her dog. She was still petting Goldie while Fred lay next to her with his nose touching my daughter's leg.

"I don't know. Maybe someone did want to scare us off the investigation." So much for thinking before opening my mouth to speak. I knew it didn't make much sense the minute I'd said it. "Or maybe it was just a burglar. I'll have to check to see if the camera pointing at the driveway was working long enough to catch the perp going toward the barn and I'll look to see if anything was taken when we get back."

"All the more reason we need to check out that list I gave you, Dad," Allie said while stroking the fur on Goldie's head.

If only she knew I was already working on it. However, she didn't need to know that

what I was planning to do next was illegal.

Chapter Twenty-seven

"I COULD BUY THE computer," Allie said when I explained my new plan to get remote access to a dry ice vendor in Sedalia. Unlike the one I'd bought on Facebook Marketplace, I needed a way to get my hands on a computer that couldn't be traced back to me. I had chosen the Sedalia vendor from her list because they gave discounts to science teachers. We were having coffee at Fido's. Well, I was having coffee. She had some kind of cappuccino topped with whipped cream and chocolate sprinkles while Goldie and Fred sat quietly, waiting for the server to bring them a doggie treat.

I took a sip of my unadulterated coffee, put the cup down, and looked at my daughter before answering. Her hazel eyes burned with the excitement of the chase. "I can't take the chance that my scheme of buying a used computer to hack with is foolproof. Your mother would never forgive me if they somehow traced my hacking back to a computer you bought. It would ruin your future. Even if they didn't put you in jail, you would never get into a good grad school or find a decent job."

Allie lowered her eyes and looked into her cappuccino as though the chocolate chips were some kind of tea leaves. "I've been thinking of dropping out."

I started to take a sip of my coffee and froze before the cup touched my lips. "What?"

Allie sat straight in her chair and crossed her arms. "It's not worth it to spend all that time

and come out owing thousands that I'd never be able to pay back."

"What if I helped you with the tuition?"

Allie went back to studying the chips in her cup. "It's the room and board I borrow money for. My scholarships pay the tuition. Besides, we both know you don't have that kind of money, Dad, so let's not go there." Her sad look reminded me so much of her mother when she'd told me to leave.

Suddenly, I felt like a huge failure. I wanted my daughter to get the education I'd always wanted. It had taken me years to work my way through college. Supporting a family and going to school had been nearly impossible. If I hadn't gotten a job at a software firm that paid the tuition for the last years of school, I'd probably still be pounding nails.

"Don't take it so hard, Dad. I've been thinking I might get a part-time job with Dr. Steadman until I decide what I want to do with my life. I'm sure Bonnie will let me and Goldie stay with her until then. In the meantime, we need to find out who's been killing county commissioners and pass it on to Kelly, so she gets the detective job."

"I don't want you doing anything that would ruin your future, so don't even think about buying that computer. Besides, I think I know how to get that list without hacking."

"Oh?"

I waved the server down before answering. "Sometimes the obvious choice is staring us right in the face."

Our server finished taking an order from another customer before coming over to our table. "Those two are so well-behaved," she said giving Goldie and Fred a biscuit.

"Could you put my daughter's cappuccino in a to-go cup?" I asked. "I just remembered that I need to be somewhere."

Allie looked at me as though I'd told her to go to her room.

"I know how to solve our little problem, kiddo, but I need to do it now before it's too late; then we can talk about your loans."

• • • ••• • ••

"I think Allie's plan to let her boyfriend do it would be better," Bonnie said as I pulled into the parking lot of the compressed gas vendor in Sedalia. We had stopped at home so I could download an app on my smartphone that would sniff out wireless routers. When Bonnie heard about my new plan, she insisted on driving us. I explained to her and Allie that I could avoid being tracked by my ISP if I hacked the vendor's computers from their routers. Most businesses had wireless routers because they wanted Wi-Fi for their phones and security cameras. I thought it would be best to simply try to get to their computers by connecting through their routers. From there I could look at their invoices and get a list of who bought dry ice around the time Maddie was murdered, but now I wasn't so sure.

The building needed some serious maintenance. It was obvious they cared more about their wholesale customers than walk-in retail buyers. I could see a middle-aged woman through the front plate-glass window, sitting behind a long counter, staring at her computer monitor with a bored expression on her face. There were several posters of the products they sold on the wall behind her and a calendar with a picture of a golden retriever fetching a stick. She didn't look up when we pulled in.

Allie was sitting in the backseat with Fred and Goldie, and saw her chance to speak up. "Don't you think that clerk is going to wonder what we're all doing in the car when you're using your Wi-Fisniffing app?"

I turned to my daughter, who had been petting my dog, "I didn't think there'd be a big window with someone watching us. What do you suggest?"

"I still think we should ask Aadesh to do it. He won't get caught, he's too smart for them."

I shut off the engine and unbuckled my seat belt so I could look my daughter in the eyes. "Hacking is a federal offense, and I can't let him ruin his life over this. There is so much of that going on right now that the government will nail anyone they catch to a cross. They would also crucify everyone involved, which includes you, Allie. I'd never be able to live with ruining your life."

Bonnie gasped and turned white. "Oh, my God, Jake. Do you really think it would come to that?"

"No. Natalie wouldn't let me live that long if Allie got arrested because she tried to help."

"Not you, Jake--Allie." She turned toward my daughter. "Please don't do anything that could get you into trouble."

I didn't know whether to be hurt or thankful that Bonnie had changed her mind about the hacking. I also didn't see any Wi-Fi devices showing up on my phone's app. "So, now that that's settled, does anyone have an idea for a plan C on how to get the information we need? If they have a router, it's hard-wired, so plan B is out the window."

．．．．．．．．．．．

"I'm wondering if you can help me," I said to the woman at the counter after entering the store with Fred on a leash. Allie had seen the calendar behind the clerk and suggested the perfect cover. She said that a dog, especially a golden, would help break the ice.

The clerk didn't look up at first and sat staring at her computer screen with narrowed eyes. I began to doubt the wisdom of using Fred.

"What a beautiful dog," she said. The minute she looked up from her screen and saw Fred, her frown was replaced with a huge smile.

"Thank you," I said, petting Fred on the head. He simply sat there, smiling, making me wonder if he understood the compliment.

"If you wait a minute, I have some doggy treats in the back. I'll go get the big boy one." She didn't give me a chance to answer and disappeared. I turned the monitor slightly and noticed she was still logged in. She had been browsing Facebook in one window with Excel open in another, and her email in a third. She must have been entering data into a spreadsheet before opening the Facebook window. I grabbed her mouse, clicked on the spreadsheet window, and saw that it was a spreadsheet of purchases. Could it be that easy?

"Let me know if you hear her coming, Freddie," I said, reaching for the woman's wireless keyboard. He looked up at me as if I'd just spoken Chinese.

The spreadsheet was for sales of the current month. I needed one before Maddie was murdered, so I clicked on a file folder icon in the task tray and saw a directory labeled "invoices." I clicked on it and hit paydirt. There was a file with the .xlsx extension for every month. I opened a new email addressed to myself and attached a couple of the files dated before Maddie's murder, then hit Send just as Fred barked.

"Here you go big boy," she said before freezing. I had replaced the keyboard and stepped away from the counter before she saw me, but I didn't have enough time to turn the monitor back to its original position. I started to mutter something when Allie came in with Goldie.

Goldie still had a bandage around her waist, but it didn't stop her from going straight for the clerk, who still had the doggie treats in her hand.

"Dad, Bonnie is having some kind of attack. I think you better check on her," she said, loud enough for the clerk to hear. I didn't waste a minute and rushed toward the door with Fred. Allie wasn't far behind.

• • • • •• • • • • •

How did you know I was in trouble?" I asked my daughter after I'd discovered that Bonnie was okay and the whole charade had been an act.

Allie exchanged a look with Bonnie and wiggled her eyebrows before answering. "We saw through the window what you did at the computer,

and when the clerk looked like she was ready to call the police, I decided you needed help."

I smiled but found myself speechless as I backed out of the parking lot and into traffic.

Chapter Twenty-eight

ALLIE WENT WITH BONNIE to her house to make us some lunch while Fred and I went to check my email. I was thinking about the best way to write the SQL program I needed to cross-reference our suspect list with the people who'd purchased dry ice and realized it had been years since I'd done that kind of programming. I'd have to download the free version of MySql before I could do anything.

I had no sooner started the download of the software when Fred barked at me. He hadn't eaten since breakfast, and his bowl was empty, so I let the files download while I refilled his doggie bowl from a fifty-pound bag of food.

My cell phone started playing Beethoven before I could get back to my computer. It was a text from Kelly. She wanted to meet at Fido's, and to come alone. The text was marked urgent.

I never could understand why people left a text if the message was urgent, so I called her back, only to have the call go into voicemail. "Be a good boy for a bit while I go meet Kelly," I said to Fred. He didn't even bother to look up from his bowl as I closed the door and headed over to Bonnie's.

My truck had been acting up lately, so I convinced Bonnie to let me use her Jeep. She only had one condition: that I left her and Allie at Wal-Mart while I met with Kelly.

· · · ●·●·● · · ·

Kelly was sitting at our favorite table reading something on her phone and didn't see me enter. "Hi, gorgeous," I said while taking the chair opposite her.

She hesitated before looking up from her phone, although I could see she was just staring and not really looking at it.

"Teller had a call from Dr. Steadman about you and the girls bringing in Goldie. The good doctor was worried someone was abusing the dogs," she said without responding to my compliment.

"You're kidding!"

"Teller had a good laugh at that when he told me, and made some remark about the only animal abuse Jake Martin could be guilty of is feeding his dog too much people food. Who do you think would do such a terrible thing, Jake?" she asked, taking a sip of the chocolate mocha that had been sitting to the side of her phone.

I tried not to laugh at the mustache the mocha left on her upper lip. "My first guess is that it was that redneck, Carl. He must have discovered the GPS tracking device I put on his truck."

She put down her cup and wiped her upper lip. I felt the temperature drop. "I thought I told you it was illegal to use one of those without the owner's knowledge."

"Don't cops do it all the time?" I asked.

"Not without a warrant and certainly nothing homemade," she said, reaching over the table to place a hand on my arm. "You know I'd do anything for you, Jake, but you went a little too far this time. I can't keep giving you information on Teller's case. If word ever gets out that you placed a GPS tracking device on his truck he'd have my badge in a heartbeat."

"Sorry, Kell. It won't happen again. We've given up on trying to prove Teller wrong, and for the record, Goldie is doing a lot better–if you count eating and chasing Fred as a sign." I tried not to show any tells that I was lying about having given up proving that Maddie had not killed herself but found myself unable to look Kelly in the eyes when I said it.

She slowly removed her hand from my arm. I could feel her eyes burrowing into me. "Jake, I appreciate what you and Bonnie have been trying to do for me, but you're wasting your time. Blood is thicker than water, and Bennett is never going to give me the promotion."

"Sorry." I was beginning to hate that word.

"Don't be. I really love you for trying to help me out. Why don't you come over to my place later and let me make it up to you? Mom is up in Lee's Summit tonight, visiting a friend, and I have a recipe for catfish I've been dying to try."

I'd finally found the nerve to look at her and was surprised to see her smiling. Had she forgiven me? "Can I bring Fred? I think he misses you."

Her police radio went off before I could say more. "Ten-fifty on Lost Valley Road. Any officer in the vicinity, please respond."

"Can you take care of the check, Jake? There's been an accident," she said, and got up, leaving her mocha unfinished while speaking into her radio.

"No problem, and I'll call you later to see what time Fred and I should come over," I said as she rushed out the door.

· · · ● ● ● ● ● · ·

"Did you leave your door open, Dad?" Allie asked as I parked by my house. I had picked her and Bonnie up at Wal-Mart after leaving Fido's.

"No, I'm sure I locked it when we left," I answered when I saw that my front door had been kicked in.

I turned off the ignition and was out of the Jeep before Allie could say more. "Fred? Where are you, boy?" I shouted as I ran into my house.

He answered with a loud bark from the bathroom. I ran over, opened the door, and was greeted by sixty-five pounds of fur, almost knocking me over. "What were you doing in there?" I asked, kneeling down to his level. He proceeded to lick my face as if I were some kind of treat.

"You better come over here," Allie said while Fred was beating his tail against the hardwood floor. She was standing at my desk in the corner of my living room.

One glance in her direction, and I knew what had happened.

My laptop looked like it had been used for batting practice. Someone must have broken in while we were gone and destroyed my computer. There were also papers from the filing drawer in my desk all over the floor.

Bonnie was just coming into the room, and froze upon seeing the carnage. "Do you think it was Carl?" she asked.

"My money's on someone at the dry ice store," I answered. "Why else would they want to destroy my computer?"

Allie let out a small yelp. "Someone must have figured out that you got a copy of their spreadsheets," she said as she started to record the mess around my desk with her phone.

"Yeah, but on second thought, anyone who knew anything about computers would wonder if I had backed up those files. They would have taken my laptop to see if I have a cloud backup service."

"Can you check if your cloud files were accessed from your phone?" Allie asked.

"I could if I had a cloud account," I answered. "I use the cheap version of Dropbox. I email important files to myself and backup everything else to a USB drive," I said, wondering if someone had found my book of passwords or the USB drive. I had so many passwords and had to change them so often that I kept them in a little notebook in my desk with the drive.

I opened the email app on my phone and checked if the email with the attached files had been deleted. The mail I sent myself from the vendor's computer was still there, then I checked my desk.

I shook my head, feeling relieved when I saw my notebook and drive where I had left them. My email account hadn't been hacked. Whoever ransacked my office must not have realized I didn't use the keyboard drawer for the keyboard, even though I had no use for one with a laptop computer. "The email is still there, so maybe it was Carl. He strikes me as the kind who would think that destroying my laptop would get rid of any incriminating evidence."

Allie sat cross-legged on the floor to hold her dog and keep Fred from licking Goldie's bandage. "Did you delete the send message when you emailed yourself from the dry ice vendor's computer?" she asked.

"No, I didn't have time, but if it was the clerk at the office, she should know that destroying my computer wouldn't stop us from having her spreadsheets."

Bonnie forced a laugh, then spoke up. "Unless she's in it with Carl. But a better question is are you going to call Kelly and report the break-in?"

I hesitated before answering, trying to decide how much I should tell Kelly.

Allie looked up from comforting her dog and sighed. "You can't tell her about the files," she answered. "We didn't exactly get those legally."

"Let me think about it before I call her," I answered. "In the meantime, you two need to get Goldie out of here before Fred licks her to death."

Chapter Twenty-nine

FRED WAS SLEEPING AT my feet by the time I'd set up an old desktop I had in my storage shed. It took me several hours to bring it up to date with the current Windows operating system and a MySQL database. I used the time to feed Fred and tell him how lucky he was to have been locked in the bathroom and not kicked like Goldie had been. When I was finally able to download the spreadsheet, insert the data into MySQL, and run my query, he had fallen asleep, but he awoke when I yelled, "Got you!"

"Not you, Freddie," I said, reaching down to pat him on the head. "It's the killer I found. At least, I think I did. Seems I was wrong. Stephanie *did* kill her mother after all." I didn't waste any time and picked up my phone.

"Do you have any idea what time it is, Jake?" Bonnie asked.

I looked at the time on my computer's icon tray. "Twelve thirty, according to Windows, but I thought you would like to hear what I found when I cross-referenced our list of suspects with the people who bought dry ice the day Maddie was murdered."

I could imagine Bonnie raising her eyebrows with a slow smile building on her face. "Okay, you got my attention, but let me find my glasses before you tell me."

Why she needed glasses to write it down was an enigma to me but I waited until she came back online. "Are you ready?" I asked.

"Enough, already. Who is it?"

"Stephanie Travers--Maddie's daughter."

"I know who Stephanie is, Jake. I'm wide awake now. But why would she kill her own mother?"

"My guess is to get the inheritance."

"I suppose, but then who broke into my barn and your house? I can't imagine Stephanie doing that, she's too far along."

I heard my daughter in the background. "Is that Dad?" We must have woken Allie.

"Well, you've managed to wake everyone except Tiger and Goldie, so why don't you come on over, and I'll put on a new pot of coffee?" Bonnie said before hanging up.

• • • •• • • • • •

Both women listened to me explain how I'd come to the conclusion that Stephanie killed her mother. Fred was checking
out Goldie, who just wanted to sleep. Neither one of the dogs
were interested in what I had to say.

Allie was all ears while Bonnie put down her coffee, and
added more sugar before yawning when I went into the details
of my SQL query.

"I don't see how that proves anything, Jake," Bonnie said.

"She's right, Dad. Didn't you say Stephanie was a science
teacher?" Allie added.

"Yeah?"

My daughter copied Bonnie and reached for the sugar bowl.
It seems they didn't appreciate coffee without some kind of
helper. "Well, my fifth-grade teacher used to show us all kinds
of experiments with dry ice. She could have bought it for her
class," she said, adding two teaspoons of sugar to her cup.

Bonnie took a sip of her brew and made a sour face. "I don't
see her lifting that highboy to put it on top of the blocks of
ice. Even if she could, which I doubt, she's too far along to lift
anything that heavy." She finished with a smile on her face as
if she had just answered a trivia question correctly.

"She must have had help," I answered without being able to make eye contact, hoping she couldn't see the doubt on my face.

"Like Carl?" Allie offered.

"That would explain why he was at the auction," Bonnie said, getting up to empty her coffee in the sink before rising out her cup. "I wonder if that's why he ran us off the road and kicked Goldie?"

"Maybe he broke into your house, too? I'm so happy we weren't there at the time." Allie was rocking back and forth in her chair, showing the classic signs of stress. I'd have to find a way to calm her down.

"I doubt if he'd have broken in if we had been home. I'm only glad he didn't hurt Fred the way he did Goldie." Everyone at the table looked over at Goldie and Fred, who were now sound asleep by the refrigerator. I had to smile; Fred had his big paw over Goldie's shoulder while Tigger was snuggled between the two goldens. It made me wonder how anybody could hurt either one of them.

I put down my cup and turned to Bonnie. "Something tells me that whoever broke into Bonnie's barn wasn't the same person who broke into my house. That person went out of his way to put Fred in the bathroom, whereas whoever broke into your barn had no feeling for dogs."

"How do you know it was a he?" Allie asked. Leave it to the younger generation to correct my bias.

Bonnie crossed her arms and snickered. "It's a figure of speech, Ms. Steinem."

"Who?" Allie asked.

I blinked. I appreciated Bonnie defending my word choice but my daughter had no idea who Bonnie was talking about.

"Oh, forget it. She was before your time. The important thing is that whoever broke into my barn and your house must have been looking for something. I don't think breaking your laptop was part of a random burglary. They wanted what they thought was on it. Is there any way they could see we're on to them?"

"Not unless they can get into my email, and I have that protected with two-step verification," I answered.

Bonnie raised her hands in surrender. "Whatever that is. I'll take it as not likely."

"It's... ow! Why did you do that, Dad?" I'd kicked Allie under the table, knowing Bonnie wasn't interested in a discourse on ways to protect digital information.

Bonnie laughed and went on, "In that case, let's assume whoever destroyed your laptop doesn't know about the vendor list or that you think Stephanie killed her mother, not that Allie and I think it was her."

"Well, if Stephanie didn't do it, there is someone we never considered. She wasn't a match for my query, but I saw that she was looking for dry ice when I looked at her search history on the computer in the nursery. She could have used Stephanie's name when she bought the dry ice."

Bonnie tilted her head and leaned forward in her chair. "She? You really think a woman could lift that highboy?"

I also had Allie's attention. She stopped fidgeting and sat straight in her chair, waiting for me to answer.

"Like I said, she must have had help doing that but think, who else would have known about the nursery?"

Bonnie looked at me blankly, but Allie's eyes lit up. "The realtor?"

"Gloria must have found the room and computer when she inspected the house. I think we need to talk to her, and I'm going to need your help," I said, looking at my daughter without blinking.

Chapter Thirty

GLORIA WAS LATE, AND the dogs wanted out, so I asked Allie to take them for a walk around the property while I waited in my truck.

Gloria finally pulled up to the house just as Allie slipped out of sight. I waited while Gloria yelled into her phone to whoever she'd been talking to. "I don't care what he knows. Just do it," she said to the person she'd been yelling at before putting her phone into an expensive-looking purse after stepping out of her Escalade. Of course, the purse could have been a cheap thrift store find for all I knew about purses, but I remembered Bonnie remarking about how much Gloria's purse had cost, so like the rest of her attire, I assumed it was expensive. I'm sure the shoes she wore had not been bought at Payless Shoes either.

"I hope this won't take long, Jake. I have to meet a real client after I hear what you have to say that is so important."

"Like I told you on the phone, I don't think Ms. Summers committed suicide. I believe she was murdered, and I know how."

"So, why call me? Isn't this information you should give to your girlfriend, the sheriff's deputy?"

"I need to show you something before I do that."

She forced a smile, but couldn't look me in the eyes. "I appreciate that. It's hard enough selling a house someone died in, and it's even worse if they were murdered in it, but I don't know what you can possibly show me, or have you forgotten I'm the listing agent? We've been all through the house, taking pictures for the website. Wouldn't you be better off asking the owner of the house? Not that Stephanie would know who killed her mother. Oh, wait... You think she did it, don't you?"

I smiled, knowing from her response that she must not know I was on to her. "Shall we go inside? A picture is worth a thousand words, or so they say," I said, holding the door open for her.

Her phone dinged as we entered the parlor. She went straight for one of the Queen Anne's that hadn't sold at auction and pulled out her cell phone. Maddie had put two of the chairs facing each other with a glass-topped coffee table between them. I sat down facing Gloria, who was now scrolling through what I assumed were her messages. "Let me cut to the chase, Gloria. I found the hidden room in the attic."

"A hidden room? And what does that have to do with me?" she said, looking up from her phone.

I had her attention. "I saw the search history on Maddie's computer, too. At first, I couldn't fathom why anyone would be interested in dry ice, but when I took my truck into the body shop to have a dent removed, and I saw the body man use dry ice, it hit me. The dry ice pellets he used evaporated without a trace. That's when I realized the killer must have used dry ice to prop up the highboy and looked for someplace to buy it after shooting Maddie," I said. Then I had another thought, "or maybe you bought it before you shot her, in which case, it was premeditated murder."

Gloria's fingers turned white as they tightened their grip on her phone, and she finally turned all her attention toward me. "You don't think I had something to do with all this, do you? I know nothing about a hidden room or computer. If you or your girlfriend checked, you must know I never bought any dry ice in Sedalia."

"I never said the vendor was in Sedalia."

Eyes that had been blazing, suddenly dimmed as Gloria lowered her gaze, "Where else would you look?" she asked with a slight crack in her voice after a few seconds. "I can't imagine getting it here in Truman. Besides, I'm sure I have an alibi for whenever you say I bought the dry ice. When I'm not showing property, I'm in my broker's office. There are several other agents who will vouch for me."

"Carl already did."

Her lip curled into a smirk. "I think you've been smoking something, Jake."

"When I saw he'd purchased two ten-pound blocks on the day of the murder, I confronted him, and he said he bought them for you. I assume you told him they were for an open house you claimed to be showing." She didn't need to know I was fishing. I hadn't seen Carl since the night I'd tracked down his truck. I had made an educated guess about the open house, knowing it wasn't unusual for relators to put out some snacks.

She smiled as if she knew I was lying. "Nice try, Jake, but why would I use dry ice at an open house? Anything that needed to be kept cold would simply go in the refrigerator."

"Luckily, Carl has the IQ of a snail, and didn't realize that."

"Even if he did buy it, what does that prove? I had no reason to kill Ms. Summers," she said, her voice raising several decibels. I started to see the holes in my lie and knew she did, too.

"I found the birth certificate for you and your twin sister, and her grave. I know Maddie was your mother, and abandoned you at birth because she blamed you for the death of your sister. It must have really hurt when you discovered the old nursery your mother kept in the attic. I assume you found it when you were inspecting the house?"

Her façade changed, and her eyes glazed over with rage. "The old bat didn't realize the agent she called to sell her house was the daughter she'd put up for adoption forty-two years ago. How could you not recognize your own daughter?"

I had hit a nerve, and suddenly felt bad for her. "I'm sorry, Gloria. I know how you must have felt. I always got the impression my mother didn't want me either."

She simply stared at me with a vacant look. For a slight moment, it looked as if she might even care, but whatever empathy I'd seen was gone as soon as it came. "She said that she couldn't look at me when I was a baby. I reminded her too much of my twin sister who died in the fire. She could only save one of us, she said, and so I should be grateful it was me. She didn't even apologize for putting me up for adoption. She should have begged me not to shoot her, but she insisted it had been for the best."

I was thinking about calling Kelly when we both froze as the front door banged open. A second later, Teller burst in, holding his service pistol. He walked over to Gloria and bent down to kiss her cheek, keeping his gun pointed at me. "Sorry I took so long to get here. Is this the creep who's on to us?"

Gloria got up from her Queen Anne chair, nostrils flaring. "He saw my search for dry ice on Maddie's computer, and figured out why we bought it, but I don't think he's shared that with his girlfriend yet. But, even if he did, you're in the clear. He thinks Carl was my accomplice."

"Well, in a way, he was. I did pay him to harass Jake, hoping he'd back off. I guess I'll have to silence him, too."

She turned to me, smiling wickedly, "Give me your phone, Sherlock. I need to see who else might know about us so Josh can quiet them as well."

I tried to think of how I could warn Allie and Bonnie if Gloria should discover their numbers on my phone as I reached into my pocket to retrieve it. As I started to pass it over, then dropped it, pretended to stumble, and stepped on it.

Teller cocked his gun and leveled it at me, "Nice try, Jake. Now, back off so I can remove the SIM card. You're right about Carl's IQ, but I'm a lot smarter. When I find who you shared this little secret with, I'll make sure they don't tell anyone else."

That explained his sudden entrance. He had been listening on the front porch through the door. He must have been who she was talking to on the phone when she arrived. I thought about picking up the phone and throwing it at him when we all heard the distinctive sound of a police siren outside and saw flashing red and blue lights through the window.

Teller took his eyes off me to look out the window. Without thinking, I kicked as hard as I could, catching him off guard and knocking the gun from his hand just as the door crashed open and Fred and Kelly ran in. Teller never saw Fred coming. Fred probably would have ripped out his throat if I hadn't grabbed his collar while Kelly kicked the gun out of his reach.

· · · ●· ● ●· · ·

"How did you know to show up when you did?" I asked Kelly, who was now smiling. Her arm was draped over my daughter's shoulder. Allie had Allie come in with Goldie after Deputy Charlie led Teller and Gloria away in handcuffs. The sheriff and his deputy had shown up seconds after Kelly had barged into the house with Fred.

"I called Kelly when I saw Teller crouching at the front door," Allie replied. "The dogs and I had just come back from our walk, and I saw him listening and checking his gun. That's when I knew they must have been on to you and called for help."

Kelly was still hugging my daughter when she answered. "She was also smart enough to record it all on her phone after calling me."

Allie's chin dropped when she lowered her head. "I knew it was your word against theirs, so the dogs and I snuck up to the window after Teller barged in. It was all I could do to keep them from going after him, but I did manage to put my phone in record mode."

Our little chat was cut short when Bonnie came into the house, her face was swollen and red. "Are you guys okay?" She was looking at Allie and the dogs, but I guess she meant me, too.

"We are now, thanks to Allie, here," I answered.

Bonnie started to say something when Bennett interrupted. He shifted his gaze towards me, shaking his head. "Can't keep your nose out of my investigations, can you, Jake?"

"Sorry," I said, hooking my thumbs into the beltless loops of my jeans, "but you accepted Teller's statement, and I knew you would never buy my theory on how Maddie's murder was made to look like a suicide."

Bennett raised his hand to rub the back of his neck. "It's a good thing your daughter showed me her recording, or I wouldn't believe he was involved either," he said, looking her way momentarily, before turning back to me. "So, tell me, Jake, just how did you come to that conclusion?"

"Well, the thing that had me puzzled was how someone could have killed Maddie and left the room. Bonnie and I couldn't find any hidden doors in the walls, ceiling, or floor, and the only window in the room had been locked and painted shut years ago. The paint seal would have been broken if it had been opened.

"It wasn't until I took Bonnie's Jeep to the body shop that it hit me. Well, the method of blocking the door to the bedroom didn't come until much later when I took my truck in, but my subconscious must have realized the dry ice they used to remove dents at the body shop was how the killer had blocked Maddie's bedroom door. He sat the legs of the highboy on blocks of dry ice and let them melt. The front legs were next to a space heater, so that ice melted first, causing the dresser to fall over and block the door.

"If he had used regular ice, it would have left a puddle. Frozen carbon dioxide was perfect because when it melts, all it leaves is a cloud of carbon dioxide. It was that gas that killed the bugs we found along the baseboard.

"Once I realized how the murderer had killed Maddie, all I had to do was find out who had access to the dry ice, which turns out to be just about everyone. I can't believe how many people use that stuff in everything from paintless dent removal to fumigation and sandblasting, and of course, to keep things cold. It's that last application that led me to our killer."

Bennett scratched the stubble on his chin. "Well, that all makes sense, but who killed our other commissioner? Or did my sorry excuse for a nephew get that one right by calling it a suicide?"

"My guess is he was on to Gloria, so she had Teller take care of him, too."

"Your guess, Jake? I'll need more than that to close the case."

Kelly jumped in to save me just in time because I didn't have a clue if someone had killed Morgan, or if he'd taken his own life. "I'm sure the DA will get Josh to confess to that one if she offers him life instead of lethal injection."

Bennett seemed to consider it, "I hope you're right, Sergeant. My sister might even speak to me again if he gets life instead of lethal injection."

· · · ● · ● · ● · ·

Bennett stood on Maddie's porch, watching as Bonnie and Allie drove away. "I suppose you heard about Maddie and me," he said to Kelly, who was standing at my right side, with Fred sitting at my left.

"That's just a rumor as far as I'm concerned."

"Still, she didn't deserve to die that way, and I'll miss her."

"I agree. It's nothing to die for. I'm just glad Allie recorded Teller and Gloria," she answered with a huge grin on her face.

He paused for a moment, took a deep breath, and exhaled before continuing, "I'm sorry I doubted you, Sergeant."

"All water under the bridge, Sheriff."

He tried to look her in the eyes, but he couldn't. He shifted his weight from one foot to another. "I got the letter from the Highway Patrol yesterday. They are asking for a recommendation before making you an offer. I'll give you one if that's what you really want, but before I do, I want you to know that I'm sorry for putting that idiot of a nephew before my most competent officer. I hope you'll reconsider. The job of a detective is yours if you want it."

Before Kelly could reply, Fred barked his approval.

About the Author

RICHARD HOUSTON WORKED AS a carpenter for 20 years while taking college classes whenever he could. After earning a bachelor's degree in math, he spent the next 25 years as a successful software engineer. Although he found success in those professions, he always dreamed of writing a novel. He honed that craft by taking every creative writing class he could. Somehow his poems and short stories usually had a dog as a major character. Richard now lives and writes at his lake home in Missouri where he and his wife are raising their granddaughter, two dachshunds, and a rescue dog that is mostly Golden Retriever.

Books by Richard Houston

Please follow me at Amazon and Bookbub if you would like to be informed of any new releases, and don't forget to leave a review while you're at it.

Made in United States
North Haven, CT
29 May 2023

37135267R00135